THE BOYS AND THEIR MOTHER

Other Books by Keith W. Jennison

The Boys
and Their Mother

by

Keith W. Jennison

New York · The Viking Press · 1956

Acknowledgment is made to *McCall's*, which
published Chapters I, III, XI, and to *Reader's
Digest*, in which Chapter VI appeared.

Library of Congress catalog card number: 56-6284

38045

Printed in the United States of America by
American Book–Stratford Press, Inc., New York

To the boys' grandparents
Clark, Louise, Harold, and Emma

THE BOYS AND THEIR MOTHER

EMILY CAME OUT of the boys' bedroom with a puzzled expression on her face.

"Something wrong?" I asked.

"You know what?" she said. "Those boys stretch right from one end of their beds to the other. Pretty soon we'll have to get longer beds."

"Those are full-size beds," I said, "and if they're going to start lopping over beds they may as well get used to it. And cheer up, maybe the boys aren't going to get any longer."

"Boys don't stop growing at fourteen and sixteen," she said, shoving a light bulb down into an almost toeless white sock. "Look at the size of this." She held up the sock. "This is for the foot of a monster."

I opened the book I intended to read. "Would you have preferred midgets?" I asked, settling myself in the chair.

"There you go," Emily said, "reading again when I want to talk. Why don't you ever talk to me?"

I put the book down. "I do talk to you," I said. "I talk to you all the time."

She snorted. "You do not talk to me all the time. You have talked to me about once a year for seventeen years. The rest of the time you not only do not talk to me, you don't even listen to what I am saying. Sometimes I think we don't know each other at all."

"Nonsense," I said. "We have lived intimately together for many years. Of course we know each other. What's the matter? Have you been reading that 'lost sex' book again?"

"No," she said. "I have been thinking."

I looked across the room. Her head was bent over her darning. "What have you been thinking about?" I asked.

"Oh," she said, "about how this raising the boys has made us see each other mostly through them. Sort of— well, sort of like a triangle without any hypotenuse. You know, with the boys as the right angle and you and me off at the other ends—having to go through the boys to find each other."

"Is that bad?" I said. "I thought that's what families were about."

"Certainly, but that's not all they're about. What happened to the hypotenuse?"

"It's still there. You're overestimating this not knowing each other. Why, we know each other like a book."

"Like what book?"

"That's just a phrase," I said. "Like any book."

Her answer was muffled. She was biting off the darning cotton.

"What did you say?" I asked. "If you want to hold an intelligible conversation you'd better take that sock out of your mouth."

"I said, 'Prove it.' "

"Prove what?"

"Prove that we know each other like a book. Show me the book we know each other like." She was looking at me with a pleasant but somewhat ominous smile.

She had me there. "I'd have to write it," I admitted.

Emily nodded. "Exactly what I was thinking."

"I don't think it's a book subject," I said. "Of course I could try parts of it."

"Well, why don't you?" she asked. "After all, parts of it are all we've got, and when they're finished maybe we could find out."

"Find out what?" I asked.

She started to put the sock back in her mouth. "How we got where we are."

I stared at her. "But I haven't got much of an idea where we really are."

"Neither have I," she said brightly, "but it's been quite a trip."

I got up and went into the kitchen for a match. The light over the sink wouldn't turn on. When I came back I said, "Trouble is, I wouldn't know where to start, and what's the matter with the light over the sink?"

"I've got the bulb," she said, "and why don't you start at the beginning?"

"Because I don't know what the beginning was," I said. "You start writing about beginnings and you've got to be a philosopher, and it takes either too much or too little money to make a good philosopher."

Emily shook her head. "Epigrams yet," she said. "Then why don't you write about money? We have had intimate dealings with it over the years."

I laughed. "Especially maybe when we tried to teach the boys about it."

"The blind leading the blind," she said and looked at me expectantly.

"It's been used," I said. "But you've got the right idea."

❧ I ❧

THE BOYS STARTED having trouble with money the day Chris got a quarter stuck in his throat. He was four, and while I held him up by his heels and his mother whacked him until the coin dropped to the floor, Nick, who was two, looked on in horror and howled in sympathy. When Chris regained his composure he grabbed the treacherous quarter and threw it out the window. This taught them both a lesson. If you don't want trouble with money, throw it away as soon as you get your hands on it.

Of course they soon found out that if you throw money in the right direction, such as across a candy counter, you get something back. This pastime grew so attractive that they took to appropriating any loose change they found around the house, on the assumption that they were doing me a favor by throwing it away. (Not that I, according to the boys' mother, needed any help.) This naturally resulted in our giving them allowances.

"If they're old enough to have allowances," we said, "they are old enough to do some regular work in order to earn the allowances." We figured that this would give them a basic understanding of the relationship between work and money. It didn't. They never could get the connection. Allowances were something they got as a right, and work was something they did when they had a mind to. We were getting nowhere.

Furthermore, they always spent their allowances the day they got them. One week Nick had an inspiration. With the last dime of his allowance he bought a handful of paper money. It didn't seem to bother him that the bills were light blue in color and displayed a picture of Admiral Farragut instead of the stern face of the father of his country. For the moment he was a genius and that was enough—until he tried to spend it.

We tried to be firm about the matter of not advancing sums against future allowances, but one day Chris approached me with a request so modest that I had to give in. He wanted two cents.

"What are you going to get with them?" I asked.

He explained that their friend Tony Perini, one of the neighboring farmer's many children, was going to sell him something for two cents. Tony wouldn't tell Chris what it was, but he assured him it was worth a lot more. This sounded a little confused to me, but I gave him the two cents and told him to do the best he could.

The afternoon passed and suppertime came, and the boys did not come home. I walked down to the Perinis' and knocked on the door. The kitchen was full of noise and children. Mrs. Perini stood by the stove with her three-month-old baby in the crook of her arm. I summoned our boys, and when we reached the door Chris called back, "Good night, Mrs. Perini. We'll be back for the baby in the morning."

After we had walked a few steps down the path, I said, "What's this about being back for the baby in the morning?"

"Oh, that's what we bought with the two cents," Chris said.

Nick explained. "Tony told us his mother got so mad at the baby this morning that she said she'd sell him for two cents. Tony came to us first. Aren't we lucky?"

"We certainly are," I said. "Wait till we tell your mother."

During these years their allowances were not their only source of income. There was always the tooth fairy. Whenever one of the boys lost a tooth, the fairy came during the night and put money under his pillow—ten cents for a small tooth, a quarter for a large one. This was fine until the boys heard of a friend who got a dollar for *any* tooth. They emerged from this experience with a somewhat depreciated confidence in the fairness of fairies.

The years went on, and the allowances went up, and the boys didn't seem to be learning anything about the value of money. They didn't buy any more babies, but they invested heavily in bubble gum—which they didn't chew. They simply extracted the sports cards and threw the gum away. Their closets, dresser drawers, and pockets became little museums of objects enthusiastically purchased, quickly damaged or broken, and immediately forgotten.

"Already they're teen-agers," I said to the boys' mother, "and we haven't taught them a single thing, so far as I can see, about the care and handling of money."

"Oh, I don't know," she said. "In the first place, only one of them is a teen-ager, and maybe we've taught them more than you think."

"I can't imagine what," I said. "They haven't even learned the truth of that old saying, 'A fool and his money are soon parted.'"

"We all know that," she said. "It's just that the three of you can't agree on who the fool is."

"Is that so?" I said. "Well, from now on things are going to be different."

In line with this pronouncement, I bought a handsome gray steel cashbox with a removable partitioned tray and a key. I explained that I would put five dollars in bills and silver into the box, lock it up, and hang the key on a nail in the wall. When their allowances were due they were simply to get the key, take the money, and leave a receipt. If they needed an advance for good and sufficient reasons, they were to make out a slip marked I O BOX and subtract it from their next allowances. When the money was gone I would total the slips, and if everything was in order I would replace the slips with more money. The first few days of the system were remarkable. The box was opened and checked many times. Balancing the box became a sort of a parlor game, like parchesi. I breathed a sigh of relief.

Sunday night there was no money left. We totaled the slips, and two dollars were unaccounted for. After some thought the boys' mother said, "Oh, yes, that must be the two dollars I gave to Planned Parenthood."

The three of us glared at her. "Why didn't you put in a slip?" we said.

On Monday morning I put five more dollars in the box, and when we looked that night there was not only no money, there were no slips either. The boys hadn't made any transactions, so we went to the lady of the house.

"What happened?" we demanded.

"Your father forgot to give me the first-of-the-month check when he left for the office this morning," she said, "but I thought you'd like to have some dinner anyway."

We tried the system for a while longer, but something always happened. Finally we lost the key. Luckily the box was open at the time, so the boys used it for fishing tackle; it was just the right size.

By this time we had come to the conclusion that the boys would show no real responsibility in money matters until they themselves had to earn most of what they spent. This was a logical theory, but it didn't pan out either. They seemed to be just as gay about getting rid of the dollars they earned mowing lawns or shoveling snow as they had been about the dollars they had come by the easy way. That is, they did until the summer of the bicycles.

It was a mail-order catalogue that started it. The boys found a picture and a description of a bicycle that was obviously the end of all bicycles. "Super 500—Our Finest," was the way the copy went. "Airflow tank; built-in electric horn; power-beamed headlight; heavy-duty luggage carrier; white sidewall tires; triple bonderized." It had everything. It was a dream. And it seemed only natural that so great a bicycle should have a great cost—$63.95. That made $127.90 for two. The sum was so staggering that they mentioned it in whispers, but they cut the page out of the catalogue and posted it in their bedroom. Throughout the winter there were long discussions of the bicycle's virtues.

During April they made an announcement at dinner one night. "We have decided to get the bicycles," they said.

Their mother and I looked at each other. "Fine," I said, "but how?"

They had a plan, they said. They were going to earn the money.

"That's a lot of money," I said. "Have you any idea how long it will take?"

"Till the middle of July," they said. They had it all figured out. They would work week ends at odd jobs until the golf course opened. Then they would caddy. Between them, they were sure, they could earn five dollars a week end. That was eight week ends at five dollars. When school closed they could get in so much more caddying and so many more odd jobs that they should be able to average ten dollars a week apiece.

"So by the middle of July at the farthest," they said, "we'll have enough to send for them." They were very happy when they went to bed.

"How long do you think it will last?" the boys' mother asked.

"We'll see," I said.

At the end of May they were still at it. A bankbook hung beside the page from the catalogue. Next to it there was a thermometer drawn in crayon on cardboard. The mercury climbed slowly past the dollar lines all through June. The thermometer had been lengthened twice: the first time when it was discovered that there would be four dollars' shipping charge on each bike; the second time when a lengthy study of available accessories indicated that their bikes would not really be complete without windshields and two-way chrome mirrors. The grand total was now $143.76.

When school was over they worked even harder. Week by week the red line mounted toward the goal. "Wait'll they see us on our Super Five Hundreds," they chortled.

When the last dollar was credited to the account they could hardly believe it. Friday evening we went to the bank and had a cashier's check drawn for the exact amount. When we got home the boys went into their room to make out the order blank. They stayed in there, talking in low voices, for a long time, and when they came out they were obviously troubled.

"What's the matter?" I asked. "Having trouble making out the order?"

"No," said Nick. "It's just that— You tell him, Chris."

"It's just that—" Chris started. "It's—well, we wondered what you'd think if we got three bicycles instead of two."

He stopped, looked at us, and then hurried on. "You

see, our friend Tony has had to work on the farm for his father and couldn't get paid, and if me and Nicky get bikes and he doesn't, then the three of us can't do things together any more, and we thought it would be a lot more fun if Tony got a bike too."

"What about money?" I asked.

"That's just it," Chris said. "We've got enough money. There's a Three Hundred Special in the catalogue that only costs forty-five twenty-five, and it's just like the Super Five Hundred except it hasn't got all that heavy chrome and junk all over it. We can get three Specials, just alike, for a hundred and thirty-five seventy-five."

"Plus eight dollars for shipping," Nick added.

I had to look away for a minute. "Go ahead, boys," I said. "It's a very nice idea."

As they left the room Nick said, "I'll bet those windshields and mirrors would just of cut down the speed."

The boys' mother and I didn't say anything for a while. Finally she got out her handkerchief and blew her nose. "How much more do you think they have to learn about money?" she asked.

"Not much," I said, "but there's still arithmetic. They're about four dollars short on the shipping charges."

After a minute she grinned. "I tell you what," she said. "I'll split it with you—two dollars apiece."

➤➤➤-➤➤➤-➤➤◄◄◄-◄◄◄-◄◄◄

When Emily finished reading she said, "Well, that's nice, but I see what you mean about its not having much to do with beginnings."

"Maybe I should have started with how you were born in Brooklyn and came to Vermont and we met at the Bishop's tea," I said.

"If you did that," she said, "you'd have to admit that you attracted me under false pretenses. The first time I saw you, you were turning pages for the pianist."

"And you thought I could read music."

"It was a perfectly natural conclusion," she said. "By the way, how did you know when to turn the page?"

"I watched his eyes," I said. "As the signs of desperation grew I knew we were approaching the end of the page. When he faltered and looked horror-struck, I turned."

"I have a certain sympathy for the man," Emily said. "Sometimes you make me feel the same way." She sighed. "That was a long time ago, wasn't it?"

"It was," I agreed, "and furthermore I don't think anyone cares but us."

"Maybe not," Emily said, "but you'll have to say something about how we started to get to know each other after we were married, won't you?"

"I guess I will," I said.

❧ II ❧

THE JULY DAY, which had started hot, got hotter, and the books in my sample case had turned to lead. I kept asking myself why the bookstores in New York were not closer together, and why there were so many people packed into the frantic, sweating city when there was so much room in America.

My thoughts turned to Jackson Heights, where we had taken an apartment when our second son was born. Nick was two now, and his brother four, and I could imagine them disporting themselves happily in the shady playground while their mother chatted with her friends on one of the benches under the big sycamores. A small worm of envy turned restlessly inside me as buyer after buyer decided that my books were either too literary or too popular for his customers. When a Department of Sanitation truck started to wash me instead of the street, I thought of the wading pool in the playground, and in the early part of the afternoon, when the asphalt turned soft under my feet, I knew the boys would be napping in their darkened room while their mother read quietly in the living room with the radio playing softly beside her.

Relatively speaking, I thought, the modern wife has it pretty easy. At least she doesn't have to work in the potato patch beside her husband, do laundry by hand, and make clothes for the family. The boys' mother has a fine life, I concluded, but I wonder if she really appreciates it.

The ride home on the subway that evening made a nitwit of the physicist who decreed that two bodies cannot occupy the same space at the same time, and when I walked into the apartment my spirit, as well as my suit, was in damp tatters.

The boys, clean, rosy, and sweet-smelling, were just awake enough to say good night to me, and I had closed the door to their bedroom before I took a good look at their mother.

I won't say she looked ghastly, because for her that is impossible, but in her stained blue denim skirt and spotted white shirt she looked a little like a Union camp follower after the Battle of Bull Run.

She stared at me with desperation flickering in her eyes.

"What happened to you?" I asked.

"You don't look so good yourself," she said. "And that suit just came back from the cleaners."

I went into our bedroom, stripped my suit off, and dropped it in the corner. On the way to the bathroom I said, "I have been tramping the streets of New York, carrying a ton of books, trying to make a living."

The tone of voice she answered in matched my own. "Well, what do you think I've been doing, dabbling my feet in a cool mountain brook and eating lemon sherbet?"

This was obviously no climate in which to discuss the matter, so I turned on the shower. When I was through I put on the thinnest shirt and slacks I could find and started for the kitchen. The boys' mother passed me on her way to the bathroom without a word.

In the light of my welcome home I didn't think she really deserved a tall, beautiful, cold Collins, but if you're going to make one you might as well use the other half of the lemon, so when she reappeared there was a frosty glass waiting for her.

"Did you really have a stinker of a day?" I asked after she had sat down and tasted the drink.

"Oh boy, did I not!" she said. "How about you? You looked pretty beat when you got home."

So we recited our recent indignities, trials, tribulations, and defeats. After another Collins the boys' mother said, "What about something to eat?"

"I don't know whether I can eat much," I said.

"What did you have for lunch?" she asked.

"Oh, a couple of other guys and I went to a pub and had a stew or something. It was lousy. Place was crowded and noisy. Service was terrible. What have we got?"

"Cold tongue and fruit salad," she said.

It was perfect, and afterward, while we were drinking iced coffee, I said, "You know, the trouble with you is you don't know how to organize your work. You really haven't got such a terrible lot to do, and with a little organization you could have time to do a lot of the things you really like to."

"Such as what?" she asked.

"Like reading and listening to music and maybe doing some drawing again."

Her lips set in a somewhat grim smile. "Just where during today do you think I might have found time to read? I haven't even seen the morning headlines yet."

"That's just the point," I said. "If you'd organize your job the way a man has to organize his, you'd have lots of spare time."

She gave me a long, level look and put her glass down on the table with a click.

"As I remember," she said, "you have made that statement to me twice a year for five years. How would you like to try it?"

It was plain that she was not kidding. "Any time you say," I said. "I'd be glad to."

"Tomorrow," she said quickly. "How would you like to organize the pants off my job tomorrow?"

"All right," I said. "I'll make a deal with the office. What do you figure to be doing?"

"Oh, I think I'll just lie in bed and do some of that translating from the Aramaic that I've been meaning to get at."

Suddenly I had an idea. "No you don't," I said. "Remember that special large-type edition of *Pride and Prejudice* that you claim to have been looking for? Well, you just go to New York and look for it. You'll probably have to go to only about fifteen bookstores before you run across it."

"See how the other half lives, hey?" she said. "That's not a bad idea."

The next morning was sunny, but it seemed cooler to me. The boys' mother had breakfast ready for all of us by the time I was dressed.

"You weren't supposed to do this," I said.

"It's a bonus in advance," she said. "You'll need it."

Just as the boys and I were finishing she came out of the bedroom, wearing a crisp light gray sharkskin suit and a white straw hat with a little crimson feather in the band.

"You look lovely," I said. "You look like General Johnston's wife after the Battle of Bull Run."

She looked at me suspiciously. "What's that supposed to mean?"

"Nothing," I said. "It's just something I thought of."

She swept the room with a smile. "Well, good-by, boys, see you later."

The moment she left, the boys started to howl, but I soon put a stop to that. I made Chris help me dry the dishes and gave Nick a tin cup to bang around while we finished. The boys watched, fascinated, while I whipped the beds together. When we started downstairs with the laundry basket I made them carry it. They spilled the clothes twice on the way, but it obviously didn't matter. After we had put the clothes in the Bendix we went out to the play yard. The boys joined their friends. I said hello to the ladies on the bench, walked to the far corner, propped myself up against a tree in the shade, and started to read Eric Ambler's new book.

I was interrupted from time to time by the activities

of a woman in a brown denim skirt who was having a hard time preventing two little boys from pouring sand down each other's throats, and who found it necessary to reprimand them in a voice just under a scream. Chris and Nick were playing quietly in another corner of the yard.

An hour and a quarter later I went in to take the laundry out of the machine and put it in the dryer. The same woman was regarding morosely a soapy pile of unfinished wash that had somehow burst out of the machine. As she started to pick it up a sound of frenzied crying came from the play yard. She said a few short words to herself, threw the wet, slippery mess of clothes into a set tub, and hurried out. I put our clothes into the dryer and took the boys upstairs for lunch.

I offered them poached eggs on chopped spinach for lunch, which they ate readily after a few words of encouragement. Then I wiped them off and put them to bed for their naps. At two o'clock I turned on the ball game, but I fell asleep, and when I woke up it was three-thirty. The boys were awake, but playing quietly in the bedroom. Chris had filled Nick's crib with the toys Nick liked best.

Four blocks away there was a big public playground with slides, swings, Jungle Gyms, and all sorts of things. The boys and I had a fine time, and on the way home we bought ice cream and a rubber duck. As we walked along, taking turns squeezing the duck, we caught a glimpse of the woman in the brown denim skirt plunging into traffic after a small boy who was wandering happily around in the middle of the boulevard.

When I got the boys home I put them and the duck in the bathtub. They were in their pajamas, eating chopped meat and potatoes, when the door opened and their mother came in. If anything, she looked better than she had when she had left that morning. She had blue forget-me-nots in her lapel and a fat book under her arm.

"Well," she said, "how are you all?"

"Just fine," I said. "How did it go with you?"

"I've had a lovely day. Did you really get along all right?"

"Very relaxed," I said, wiping the remains of dinner off the boys' faces. "Now kiss your mother good night, boys, and go jump into bed." Chris did as he was told, but Nick was carried in. Their mother was in the bedroom for some time. Just as she came out the doorbell rang. I answered it and let the sitter in.

"What's this?" the boys' mother asked.

"Oh, I thought we might go out for dinner," I said. "You know, little celebration."

"Had enough housekeeping, hey?" she asked.

"Not at all," I said. "We haven't been out for quite a while, and I just thought you might enjoy dinner and a movie."

She kissed me and said that she would love to go out for dinner and a movie. During dinner I described my day in detail.

"Do you mean to tell me that there was nobody in the laundry when you got there, you didn't have to wait, and the machine didn't go on the blink in the middle?"

I assured her none of these things had happened. "How did you like the subway?"

The subway had been fine, she told me. A man had given her his seat, and she had read the paper on the way in. Did I, she wondered, often give my seat to a lady?

"The question is academic," I said. "I have never had a seat, and, seeing as how my paper is squashed against the egg on my vest, I have to be content with what I can glimpse in other people's papers."

"Tell me about the play yard," she said. "How many fights did the boys get in, and did Gertie Stanhope get any news about her mother-in-law's ulcer?"

I told her that the boys had not fought at all, and that I had not exchanged so much as a word with La Stanhope. I inquired how many booksellers she had been forced to visit before she found the book she wanted.

"I went to the Melrose Bookshop first and found a copy right away," she said.

"The Melrose," I said, shuddering. "And you got out alive?"

"There was a charming elderly man there who was so sweet to me."

"Charming?" I said. "Last week he snarled at me, and next week, if I set foot in the store with a new book to sell, he has sworn to bite me. What did you do then?"

"Oh, I sort of walked around. I went into the Fine Arts Room at the Public Library, and then I looked for a place for lunch."

"What did you find?" I asked hopefully.

"Well," said the boys' mother, "I wanted to see the show at the Museum of Modern Art, and I remembered that they served lunch in the garden. It was lovely—cool and quiet. Food was good too. What did you have for lunch?"

"Eggs and spinach."

"And they ate the spinach?" Her eyebrows climbed up her forehead. "The last time I served spinach they blew it out all over the walls of the dinette. And they took their naps too? My, you are a marvel."

I shook my head. "When I think of you creeping right into the heart of the Melrose Bookshop, I must admit you are the marvel."

"Well, you also have to admit," she said demurely, "that I was trying to buy something from him, while you were trying to sell him something. I guess he reacts differently according to the circumstances."

"He hasn't got any corner on that," I said. "And now that we're admitting things, it occurred to me that while I did one batch of clothes, made the beds, and slapped a meal together, I did not do the cleaning or the marketing either."

"Or get dinner." She was grinning at me over her lamb chop.

"Well, you only went to one bookstore too," I said.

She offered me her hand across the table. "Truce, truce," she said. "What time did you say it was you took the laundry down and found nobody there?"

I told her. I also told about the woman in the brown denim skirt and the exploding laundry.

"Those machines will do that every once in a while,"

the boys' mother said. "From your description, I guess that must have been Sally Mason. Last week she was doing her husband's shirts and she put in a new little pair of red overalls. Everything came out pink."

"That's too bad," I said. "Almost any other color and he'd be able to wear them. And tell me about that place you went for lunch. It sounds a lot better than most of the ones I've been going to."

"You'd like it a lot," she said, "but I want to say one more thing about the Melrose Bookshop. Before the owner came to wait on me he was saying some awful things to a young man who was terribly hot and was carrying a very heavy bag of something."

"That was no young man," I said. "That was me. And what was so heavy in that bag was books. I told you he bit."

"Well, don't let him bite you," said the boys' mother.

"And when you rush out into traffic, please watch both ways," I said.

She looked startled. "What do you mean?" she asked.

I told her about Sally Mason and the wandering boy on the boulevard.

"Chris doesn't do that any more," she said. "And I think I'd rather face traffic than Mr. Melrose when he's in a bad mood. My, travel is a broadening thing, isn't it?"

"So is staying home," I said.

⟶≫-≫-≫⟪-⟪-⟪⟵

"I really was worried about you that day," Emily said. "I figured that that blonde from upstairs would be chasing you all over the play yard."

"She chased a lot of boys," I answered, "but they were all much younger than I was. By the way, you never told me where you got those forget-me-nots."

"So I didn't." She looked away, smiling reminiscently.

"Hmmmm," I said. "A penny . . ."

"I'll take it," she said. "But only because I'm not thinking what you think I'm thinking. After the movies that night I figured that with what you spent on the sitter, the dinner, and the movies, we all could have spent the day at Jones Beach."

"All right," I answered. "I am perfectly willing to admit that there are lots of things about the care and feeding of money I don't know, but it is not entirely my fault. Remember the 'thing'?"

"I do indeed," Emily said. "I also remember what happened when you tried to get rid of it by writing about it."

❧ III ❧

*F*OR MANY YEARS I have been aware of a certain noisome "thing" that keeps looking over my shoulder, down into my pocketbook, and separating me from amounts of so-called extra money.

I am, of course, using the word "extra" in its loosest sense. What happens is this. Every once in a while, with my creditors thrown off stride by a larger installment than usual on the current indebtedness, I find myself in possession of a sum of money which I can with reasonable safety leave in my checking (special) account for a few days. Whenever this happens, the "thing," getting its information from God knows where, springs into action, and I am immediately relieved of the exact amount of the cache. It isn't being parted from the money that bothers me, although that is bad enough. What really worries me is how the "thing" finds out so precisely what the sum is.

It all began a long time ago. When the boys were born we started a savings account for them. With the help of

various well-heeled aunts, uncles, and godparents, this
sum was built up over the years to the tidy, compared to
the boys, sum of $113.50. During the late fall of the first
year we lived in the country they slept happily in a room
that was extremely well ventilated even with the windows closed. When the January winds came whistling
through the charming old hand-hewn clapboards it was
obvious that the room had to be insulated. The estimate
for materials and labor came to $133.50. Which we didn't
have. But the boys did. One of them had had a twenty-
dollar birthday the week before.

As the years came and went it became evident that,
while we weren't exactly living beyond our income, we
did seem to be living ahead of it. We tried a series of
stern budgets designed to keep a little cash around the
house, but we gave them up. It was uneconomical to
have money. Every time there was a slight surplus in the
budget something that cost exactly that amount went
wrong with the car, which ran perfectly, with no need
for repairs, as long as we had no balance at all.

Two summers ago we made a mistake in our check-
book. What made this particular mistake remarkable was
that it appeared that we had one hundred dollars more
than we thought we had. Five minutes after the bank
confirmed this pleasant truth the cesspool backed up.
We had to have a new ditch dug and new tiling put in.
The local expert made us a special price of, naturally,
one hundred dollars.

Last fall, out of the blue, one of the trade magazines
called me to ask if I would write a piece for them. I
would be delighted, I said. I did the piece and sent it in.

They accepted it and sent me a check for three hundred dollars. I had told the boys' mother nothing about the matter, figuring I'd start wiping my glasses with ten-dollar bills and leave a trail of them around the house.

The night I got the check she met me at the station as usual, and as we were driving home she informed me that the school dentist had told her that Chris needed braces. If the job were done immediately, the dentist said, it would be short and inexpensive.

"How much?" I asked, having a talent for superfluous questions.

She told me.

I told her about my check.

"But who told the dentist?" she asked.

"It's a mystery," I said.

->>>->>>->>>-<<<-<<<-<<<-

"And you know," Emily said, "it still is a mystery. I remember later that night you said that since you'd sold one piece maybe you could sell another, so you sat down to write the 'thing' out of our lives forever."

"I can remember four nights later, when I finished, too," I said. "I went to the bathroom to wash my hands, and there was no hot water."

"And you called the contractor to find how much a

new hot-water heater would cost so you could know how much to expect to get for your piece."

"I was right, too, wasn't I?" I said.

"You certainly were," Emily said, "almost to the penny." She laughed. "How do you suppose we've gotten along as well as we have?"

"I don't call it well, exactly. You wouldn't say that a man treading water is speeding toward an objective, would you?"

"No, but think a minute. What do you really want to own that you haven't got?"

I glared at her. "Are you going to give me that health-is-wealth-and-money-won't-buy-happiness routine? I'll tell you exactly what I want. I want a Jaguar XK410 and enough money to sit around in the back yard with a Speedie-Sun-Tan collar on when there is weeding to be done."

"You do that anyway," she said with more accuracy than tact.

"I'd enjoy it more," I said stiffly.

"Well, I wouldn't," she said. "You'd be torquing and down-shifting and drifting all over the countryside, and I couldn't relax for a minute."

"Well, don't worry," I said. "I doubt if there is a Jaguar in my future."

"Talking about Jaguars," Emily said, "reminds me of the boys' bicycles, which reminds me of that mail-order catalogue. The boys were more interested in that book than in any book we ever had in the house."

"Oh, I don't know if I'd go that far," I said, "but it

certainly got more attention than that best-seller called Elementary Algebra."

"I wish they liked reading more," Emily said wistfully. "We've always had good books around, but somehow books have never made much of a dent in the boys."

We had talked about this many times before, but this time I had a real inspiration. "Maybe that's the trouble," I said.

"Maybe what's the trouble?" Emily asked.

"Well," I said, "as I remember, we were so anxious to have them grow up loving books that we used to encourage them to take books to bed with them, right?"

"Certainly," she said, "but what—?"

"Did you ever try sleeping with a book in your bed? It's hard and it's got sharp corners and—"

"Oh, shut up," Emily said. "And it leaves dents. That's not what I mean."

"I know what you mean," I said.

"I don't know whether you do or not," she said doubtingly. "It's not just books, it's music and movies and paintings."

"We shouldn't try to impose our taste," I said.

"I didn't try to impose anything," Emily said. "I just tried to show them what fun and magic there was in children's books."

"Leadership, eh?"

"Certainly."

I started laughing. "I know once when my leadership fell flat on its face."

"When was that?"

"When Chris caught me reading his comics."

"You can try to be funny about it all you like, but it is very serious," Emily said, "and I still don't believe you understand much about it."

"I'll show you how much I understand about it," I said, "in the usual way—including the ironing incident of last week."

"What ironing incident?" she asked—a little defensively, I thought.

"You'll find out." I started to leave the room, but at the door I turned around. "I know one book they'll have to read."

Emily looked up. "What book?"

"This one," I said.

❧ IV ❧

$\mathcal{J}$ HAVE CONCLUDED, with not too much thought and no professional consultation, that a boy's first considered reaction to a book is one of rejection. When this exciting new oblong object is first placed in his hands he naturally tries to eat it. When this proves to be impossible he tries to throw it. If he's lucky enough to hit his brother the first time, he feels a happy sense of accomplishment, but he soon learns that a book is an unreliable projectile. So there he is, left with an utterly useless object that won't throw straight and tastes worse than those brown squares of synthetic toast that someone is always stuffing down his throat.

Some enterprising publisher is going to corner the children's book market one day by printing *Little Black Sambo* on real pancakes or telling the story of Babe Ruth on a tape that can be unreeled inch by inch from the inside of a baseball. Until then, however, parents are going to have to do the whole job by themselves.

In our case, the boys' mother started reading to them at an age when they obviously didn't know one word from another, but they liked attention and they loved the sound of her voice. Little by little they began to associate this pleasant experience with what she held in her hands, but it was a long time before they grew daring enough to explore the inside of a book without her. *Bambi* was one of their first favorites, and when the movie was announced we could hardly wait until it came to our neighborhood playhouse. Apparently neither could a lot of other parents, because we had to stand in line before we got in. It was a long wait, and the boys' sense of anticipation far from equaled our own; they were nattering little wrecks by the time we found seats. Then *Bambi* appeared, and they started howling. They screamed without interruption for seven minutes, after which, and with the intense approval of the entire audience, we took them home.

"Well, there's one good thing about it," the boys' mother said the next day. "They won't be after us to be taken to the movies for a while."

She was right, too. They didn't come after us, we went after them. Three days later they were missing from the play yard and were finally located back in the theater, sitting, fascinated, through a performance of Carole Lombard in *Made for Each Other.*

Radio programs such as "The Lone Ranger" were a big influence on the boys' thoughts, speech, and clothes during those years. Of course the reading aloud went on too, but their mother found it increasingly hard to keep them quiet while she read to them. It began to become apparent that the best time to read to them was when they weren't feeling well. There was one year when they were packed off to bed with the first cough. My theory was that their mother did this just to immobilize them while she tried to fan the glimmering spark of reading interest in them, but she said it was medically sound anyway.

This therapy was quite successful until the boys discovered that, with the proper wheedling, they could get the radio moved in beside their beds. Once this was established, they leaped eagerly into bed as soon as they could work up a good sniffle, and spent the day listening to soap operas.

Of course once in a while they got sick enough to be absolutely defenseless. While they were both down with severe attacks of measles their mother got through almost all of Howard Pyle's *King Arthur*.

"The terrible thing was," she said, "as soon as strength enough crept back into their bodies, their little hands would slowly crawl over to the radio and there would be 'Ma Perkins.' "

The biggest fracas of all was caused by comic books. This campaign left the family as divided as the Balkan Peninsula. My point was that the boys were going to read comics anyway and I didn't want them sneaking off to the houses of friends to do so. The boys' mother was in favor of banning comics from the house entirely.

"How can you let them fill up their minds with that slop?" she asked.

"I'm not letting them," I said. "Comics are part of their time and part of their society. Let's have them around so we can at least exercise some control over what they get."

"All right, then," the boys' mother decreed. "Go ahead, control it."

The first rule I made was that there were to be no comics in the living room. The room is full of books, and I figured that in an agony of boredom they would be driven to examine the resources of our library. My mind painted a picture of a family almost as happy as the one pictured in the ads for the Encyclopædia Britannica.

It didn't work out that way at all. The boys vanished into their bedroom, read comics, and listened to soap operas at the same time. It was true that there were no comics in the living room, but there were no boys either.

I considered changing my position and heaving the comics out of the house altogether, but by this time the boys' school work was getting more demanding and there were occasional hours of the day when they were not looking at comic books, so the situation didn't seem quite so threatening. Besides, the boys' mother had discovered that a stock of comic books was a very handy thing to have around when her friends brought their children to call on her.

On one occasion I started to divide the boys' backlog of comics into two piles, one to keep and one to throw away. I was getting along fine until I began to get interested in the adventures of a certain character. I selected the successive issues that chronicled his adventures and was engrossed in my reading when I looked up to find Chris bending fondly over my shoulder.

"I didn't know you liked Joe Palooka," he said.

Some years after this incident the boys' mother, remembering the success she had had with the measles, figured out another way to capture, if not captivate, her audience. Almost every summer we made several trips to northern Vermont. The drive took us almost all day, and we didn't have a radio in the car. So, fearlessly gambling her eyesight, she started reading aloud as we drove. She picked out two volumes of Thomas Costain's *Pageant of England*. She and I enjoyed it very much, and the boys said they liked it too.

"They may not be intellectual," I said, "but at least they're courteous."

In the area of music, the boys had such a violent first love affair with "Peter and the Wolf" that for many years it was evident that nothing could replace it in their affections. We tried the "William Tell Overture" on them, but their only reaction was to shout, "Heigh-ho, Silver!" at the obvious time.

After some years of controversy their mother developed a theory. "It's because they hate me," she claimed. "They just delight in frustrating me as completely as possible."

"Oh, stop it," I said. "They do not hate you. They're just developing tastes of their own."

"They do so hate me," she said. "I know they do." Then she brightened visibly. "There's one thing about it, though."

"What's that?" I asked.

"At least they know it. I can tell they know it because they are so deliberate about it."

"What's good about that?" I asked.

"Don't you see?" she answered. "If they know they

hate their mother they won't have to pay some analyst a couple of thousand dollars twenty years from now to find it out."

"That might be funny," I said, "if it weren't so gruesome."

There did seem to be some antagonism working, though, for when the boys' mother made an occasion of taking them and any of their friends who wanted to go to a brilliant new movie version of *Romeo and Juliet*, not only were no friends interested, but on the way to the movie Chris asked, "Do you think we'll like this as well as *Blackboard Jungle?*"

Of course the fight is not over yet. Nor will it be, as long as the boys are living at home. Boys and parents being willful animals at best, I suppose the most we can hope for is a nonaggression pact. I feel that this pact is soon to be ratified by the boys' mother because on the last school holiday she was doing some ironing in the kitchen and Chris came through on his way to play ball. The radio was on, and the boys' mother was listening with complete absorption. The program was "Young Doctor Malone."

Chris listened for a minute and then said, "When did you start listening to that junk?"

->>->>->>((-((-((-

"I take it back," Emily said. "You know more about it than I thought. And how did you find out about that ironing business?"

"Chris told me," I said.

"The whole incident has been overemphasized," Emily went on with what looked like a sulk. "I was listening to the radio, but not seriously."

I kept a discreet silence.

"It was just a sort of a nice friendly voice in the background," she said.

"Don't be so defensive," I said. "Millions of women listen to soap operas all the time."

"I hope they listen better than I do," Emily said. "I'd hate to think of all those actors working so hard and not getting any more attention than I give them."

"You are probably conditioned by the first winter we spent in the house," I said. "You didn't have time to listen to the radio."

"Oh, I had time," Emily said. "It was just that my teeth were chattering so loud I couldn't hear it."

"Come now," I said. "It wasn't as bad as all that."

"How would you know?" she asked. "Sitting there in your nice warm office all day."

"I was there at the beginning," I said, "and nights and week ends."

"It isn't the same," Emily concluded. "Things like that are different for women."

⫷ V ⫸

JT WAS OLD and worn and it needed paint, but it was roomy, rambling, and beautiful, and we wanted it. We had never had a house of our own, and in the fall of 1946 there weren't many houses available within commuting distance of New York.

Chris and Nick stood beside us as we waited for the reappearance of the man we had hired to inspect the house.

"Are we going to live here?" Chris asked. "Are we?"

"We'll see what the man says," I answered.

"Which would our room be?" Nick asked. His mother told him. "There are lots of rooms, aren't there?" he said.

"There are an awful lot of rooms," she agreed.

Our inspector friend wriggled out of the crawl space under one of the additions.

"Well?" I asked.

He looked at me for a moment and then spat in the grass by his foot. "You wasn't figuring to live here for more than twenty, thirty years, was you?"

"At the outside," I said.

"She'll be all right," he said. "She's been here for better'n a hundred and fifty. She'll last. Probably last longer'n you will."

"I wouldn't be surprised," I said.

The house was, of course, occupied when we decided to buy it, and what with tenants, surveyors, banks, lawyers, and the ultimate necessity for locating someone with a fearless enough imagination to take a second mortgage, it was into November by the time we moved in.

The boys' mother and I vividly remembered Mr. Roosevelt's phrase about our generation's having a rendezvous with destiny, and the first time we walked through our house when it was bereft of furniture and a family we had a feeling we were due for an experience. We saw a hundred things that had escaped our notice on our earlier inspection. There were no floor plugs, so that the placing of lamps, radios, and appliances eventually made the house resemble a bombed-out spaghetti factory. The plaster was in far worse shape than I had thought, the windows rattled, wallpaper peeled off of its own accord, and a shoot from the wisteria vine had penetrated the floor in our bedroom. We couldn't very well teach the boys to hang their clothes in closets, because there were practically no closets. The ancient hot-air furnace was very big, but the oil burner was very small.

"Our neighbors' gardens will bloom all winter," I muttered, making a mental estimate of the probable heat loss.

But we had ten days of perfect Indian-summer weather. We arranged and rearranged furniture, had the pump checked, the furnace cleaned out, and the bottled-gas tanks filled; and we bought five hundred gallons of fuel for the oil burner. Our spirits rose higher with each fine day, and our date with destiny seemed very far in the future.

On the morning of the third Saturday in November I was awakened by a stream of wet, icy air blowing directly on my head. I quickly stuffed a sock into the broken windowpane beside my bed and turned on the oil burner. It started at once with a heartening roar. There was a cold gray northeast wind blowing, and a film of sleet had already formed on the power lines leading to the house. I looked into the boys' room. They were mounds in the middles of their beds.

The boys' mother appeared in the hall, shivering. "What's that noise?" she asked.

"What noise?"

"That grinding and whirring and thumping."

"That's the oil burner," I said.

"Is it going to make that noise all the time?"

"Only when it runs," I said.

She went into the living room and stood over a register. "There's no heat coming up," she said.

I went down into the cellar and inspected the pipes leading from the old furnace. All the dampers were closed. I opened them. When I got back upstairs the boys' mother was wriggling her bare toes. "Now there's some heat," she said.

We soon discovered that a cubic area of about three feet by four feet by six feet, directly over the register, was quite comfortable. So was the bathroom. The boys' mother got dressed in slacks, a pullover, a turtle-neck sweater, and a cardigan. Then she went to the kitchen to make muffins.

"Not," she said, "because I like muffins, but because I'm going to light the oven and I might as well cook something in it."

The boys' room was the coldest of all. The wind seemed to sift through a hundred cracks in the clapboards and holes in the plaster. With some urging they leaped from their beds and dashed for the bathroom.

When they got to the breakfast table they exclaimed over the muffins.

"They're good," Chris said. "Can we have them again?"

"Unless there are some changes around here," said his mother, "you are going to be eating them all winter."

"Can we tack our pictures up on our wall today?" Nick asked. "You said maybe we could."

"Tack up anything you want," I said. "The more the better."

They had a lovely morning. They collected, sorted, tacked, nailed, and glued. Frequently we were hammering on the same wall, they from the inside and I from the outside. I worked for hours with a calking gun and with strip insulation. While the house itself had been pronounced broom clean by the previous occupants, nothing had been said about the cellar. It was full of the most extraordinary collection of junk and trash any of us had ever seen. For the boys it was heaven. They hated to break off their decorating even for lunch, but I was glad of a respite from mine.

"Are you having fun?" I asked.

"Sure," said Chris. "It's the first place we ever lived where you let us fix our own room up."

In spite of the fact that the oil burner ran continuously, the house did not warm up, so shortly after lunch I laid a fire in the big, flat, old-fashioned fireplace in the living room. Just before I lit it I remembered to check whether the damper was open. There was no damper, and a cascade of cold air was pouring out over the hearth. The fire smoked for a while, but as soon as it started drawing properly the room warmed up quickly.

"Well, that's two warm rooms," said the boys' mother, "the living room and the bathroom. We'll get to know each other pretty well this winter." She started back to the kitchen. "I'm going to cook that bottom round roast for dinner," she said. "I know you like it rare, but I'm sure you will understand why you are going to get it well done."

I worked for an hour or so, sorting out the storm windows, a task which had been urged on me during the previous two week ends. Then I came in to warm up. When I went into the boys' room I thought I had stumbled upon the winter quarters of some sports-mad gypsies. The walls were almost entirely covered with pictures of heroes of the world of sports, from Jim Thorpe to Harry "the Cat" Brecheen. Other decorations included a green linen map of Vermont; a large, stained, four-color lithograph of "Custer's Last Stand," distributed by some beer company; two felt pennants, one advertising Yale and the other Coney Island; a large *National Geographic* map of Southern Rhodesia; and an empty pillowcase on which were stenciled the words, "I Pine for You and Bawl-Some."

"Isn't it nice?" Nick asked. "We love it here."

"Best room we've ever had," Chris added.

"Is it any warmer, though?" I asked.

The boys shrugged. "Who cares?"

"Where did you get all the new stuff?" I said.

"In the cellar," Nick said. "And there's lots more, too."

I saw that the stovepipe hole over the mantelpiece of the blocked-up fireplace had not been plugged up. "You'd better find something to put over that," I said just as the boys' mother called me from the kitchen. On the way I stopped and put some wood on the fire.

"The stove went out," she said grimly. "Did they or did they not fill the gas tanks?"

"They said they did," I answered and went outside to investigate. The atmosphere around the tanks was reeking with gas. As nearly as I could discover, something had gone wrong with the valve that connected the tank in use with the reserve tank. Both the tanks were now empty.

"I'm sure the company will be delighted to fix it on Monday," said the boys' mother when I told her. She was right.

It was raining now, an icy, driving rain that froze when it hit. The telephone and power cables had sheaths an inch in diameter around them.

"I hesitate to mention this," I said, "but I wouldn't be at all surprised if we had power failure before too long."

"That will be just peachy," the boys' mother said. "What will happen?"

"Well, first," I said, "the lights will go out."

"Candles we have," she said.

"The oil burner will stop."

"Not that we'll notice the difference," she said.

"And the water pump won't work."

"Oh," she said.

I left her with a somewhat pensive look on her face and went into the bathroom to draw a tubful of water to use for flushing the toilet if the power did go off. Not thinking too carefully about what I was doing, I turned on the hot-water tap and went back to the kitchen.

After a while the boys came to the kitchen too. "What's that big hot bath for?" Chris asked warily.

I told him.

"But why use hot water?"

"Why indeed?" said his mother. "Seeing as we won't have any more till Monday."

"No baths tonight," said the boys. They went back to their room.

"I'll call the gas company," I said. "Maybe I can get them to make a special trip."

The phone was dead.

The boys' mother came in with the roast. She held it up to me and grinned. "Looks like you're going to have rare meat tonight."

"Not that rare," I said. "As the man said, I've seen animals recover who were hurt worse than that."

"All right," she said. "You grind up a couple of pounds

of it and we'll cook hamburgers over the fire in the living room."

She turned on the radio, and I began grinding. Fifteen minutes later the power went off.

"They weren't playing very well, anyway," said the boys' mother and started lighting candles.

We built the fire up and brought the grill and paper plates and cups. We spread a red checkered oilcloth in front of the fire, started cooking the hamburgers, and called the boys.

"We found something for that hole in the chimney," Chris said.

"What?" I asked.

"You'll see," he said.

We gave the boys hamburgers and milk. "No vegetable?" Nick asked hopefully.

"Wait a minute," his mother answered. She went to the kitchen and came back with four large raw carrots.

"Oh, that's not so bad," Chris said.

After we finished we threw the paper plates and cups into the fire.

"Wow," said Nick, stretching out on the floor. "This is the life."

His mother watched the dinner dishes burn up. "You may have something there," she said. "Shall we read something?"

I read from *The Jungle Book* by the light of two candles. The boys got sleepy early. "Let's all go to bed," I said. "I want to set the alarm clock so I can get up a couple of times and keep the fire going."

"I think the boys had better use their sleeping bags," their mother said.

"Hurray!" they shouted. "We're all going to bed at the same time, and we get to sleep in our sleeping bags."

We sat looking into the fire and discussed ways and means of doing all the things to the house that had to be done. The list and our faces grew longer.

"I feel very much like the grasshopper in the fable," I said.

"Never mind," the boys' mother said. "I don't like ants."

After a while we went in to kiss the boys good night. They were already asleep, warm and happy in their heavy sleeping bags.

I looked over the mantelpiece. The stovepipe hole was covered with a moldy, flyspecked piece of cardboard, printed to look like an old-fashioned sampler. On it, in a flowery and much decorated script, were the words, "God Bless Our Home."

"He sure has, hasn't He?" I said.

She nodded slowly, then looked at me. "But if you want Him to help you with the house," she said, "you'd better get a stack of those how-to-do-it books."

>>>->>>->>>《《-《《-《《-

"One thing I've never been able to figure out about that winter," Emily said, "is why you put fixing your own window at the end of your list. That sock was there for months."

"It served as a constant reminder," I said. "You know, it was the last thing I saw at night and the first thing in the morning."

"Well, we survived," Emily said.

"We did more than survive," I said. "Just think how much stronger your moral fiber is because things were a little tough for you the first couple of winters."

"My moral fiber," Emily answered, "gets stronger in direct ratio to how warm it is kept. Nothing is gained by freezing it."

"You were never close to freezing," I said. "Of course we weren't as warm as the boys, but—"

"Only because they were always playing some game or sport," Emily interrupted. "I'll say that much for sports."

"There's a lot more to be said for sports than that."

"Then why don't you write it?" Emily said. "All you three do is sit around and talk about it."

"Sort of in self-defense, you mean?" I asked.

Emily smiled. "I have always heard it referred to as the manly art."

"That's boxing," I said.

"I know," Emily said, "but you're getting a little old for boxing, aren't you? Wouldn't you rather work out as a young writer?"

"You'll see," I muttered.

◄§ VI §►

I AM," said the boys' mother, "going to put a meter on our car. If I'm going to be a taxi driver by appointment to the young sportsmen of the county, I'd like to know how much I'd be making—if I were making anything, if you see what I mean."

I saw what she meant, all right. We live more than five miles away from the school that the boys and their friends attend, and there's a great deal of chauffeuring to do in connection with all the sports they engage in.

"*Mens sana in corpore sano*," I said. "You don't want them to be all brain, do you?"

"Of course I don't. It's just that their *mensi sanas* and *corpores sanos*, or whatever the plural is, are making a mental and physical wreck out of me."

"Oh, come now," I said. "It can't be as bad as all that."

"Just you try keeping their practice and game schedule straight for a while—football, basketball, pick-up hockey games whenever there's ice within a hundred miles of here, baseball, caddying at the golf course, fishing. Doesn't anybody ever play chess any more?"

"It's important for them to play a lot of different games," I said with what I hoped was considerable dignity.

"Why?" she asked. "Because you did?"

"That is hitting below the belt," I said, without realizing that I was being a perfect straight man.

"Aha!" She pounced. "You're so full of sports you can hardly speak without using a sporting reference."

"Sports are a very important part of my life," I said stiffly. "I learned something different from every sport I ever played. And so will the boys."

"Something different from *every* sport?" Her eyebrows went up.

"Certainly," I said. "But mostly from baseball."

"Well, tell me, then, old sportsman—I mean old sport," she said with a doubting but friendly smile on her face.

"I will," I said. "But first I am going to take a walk. I ate too much dinner."

As I passed the boys' room I stopped and listened at the closed door. I couldn't hear a sound. Fine boys, I thought, sitting in there, slugging away at their homework. I knocked and went in.

Chris was seated at his desk, designing a new thirty-thousand-seat indoor arena. "It'll make Madison Square Garden look like a chicken coop," he said.

Nick was poring over a large reference book filled with small type. "Do you know," he said, "that Yale has been playing football for eighty years, has played five hundred and thirty-four games, and won seventy-eight point six per cent of them?"

"What about your homework?" I asked.

"That's all done," they said simultaneously.

"Better be," I said in my menacing voice.

As I walked down the road I wondered how I would explain to the boys' mother exactly what I meant, and I remembered what had happened when we gave Chris a new fielder's glove a couple of years before.

He had told us a good deal about the glove he wanted, but he didn't really think he was going to get it, even though the one he had was thin and torn. He had been discouraged by the price. So had I been when the man at the sporting-goods store told me how much it was. The glove I had bought for Nick two years before was not a full-size major-league model, and I wasn't quite prepared to have a baseball glove cost almost as much as a suit did when the boys' mother and I were married. At fourteen, Chris was a big-leaguer in spirit if not in body. While it was expensive to equip the spirit so magnificently, it was, I told myself, in the nature of an investment.

"Oh, gee," he said when he opened the box. "A George Kell model, just like I wanted, with lacing across the top of the fingers. Gee, thanks." His face and voice conveyed his thanks more completely than his words, and the glove stayed on his hand for the next three hours, except during dinner. We had to draw the line somewhere.

Chris and Nick had a catch before dark, and after they

had undressed I went to the bedroom. They were both in bed, with their baseball gloves on their hands.

"It's wonderful, Daddy," Chris said. "Just exactly the one I dreamed about."

Nick looked at his own older glove with passionate loyalty. "I wouldn't trade this old glove for any new glove in the world," he said. "All broken in and everything, pocket just in the right place."

"There isn't a better glove than mine anywhere," said Chris. He brought the glove up to his face and nuzzled it. "See how good it smells."

It did smell good, and I told him so as I handed it back to him. "This'll last me for a long time, won't it?" he asked, his voice coming from behind the glove, sounding muffled. I said it would.

He studied the glove again. "Made in America," he said. "My glove was made in America." He laughed. "So was I. So was my brother." Then, as an afterthought: "Baseball too. All made in America."

"You're pretty sound products," I said. "Better turn off the light and get some sleep."

I thought about this conversation as I walked along the dark road, and wondered how well the boys would discharge the responsibility this label put upon them. Certainly the game of baseball was doing all right, and I couldn't remember a time when the boys wouldn't rather be playing it than anything else. I remembered showing them how to catch and throw, how to hold a bat and stand at the plate, how to handle their feet and bodies when they went after a ball hit on the ground. But mostly they taught themselves, learned from going to games, studying pictures in sports magazines, and watching games on TV.

What a huge part of their lives baseball has been, I thought. With the world of the home and the world of school, baseball was really their third world, and the one which, on a conscious level, they probably liked the best. This worried me a little, and I began to think back to see if I could discover what effect the world of baseball was having on the boys.

We'd never lived in an area that had Little League baseball, so the games the boys played in were pick-up affairs, involving, as I have said, a good deal of chauffeuring by the boys' mother, and some telephoning by myself to inform parents that their wandering shortstop would be right home. Baseball, I realized, had been the first unsupervised team game the boys played, the first social experience in which they had had to submit to the discipline and authority of their contemporaries. The rules they followed were not imposed by parents or teachers, but by themselves. Not that this prevented the rules from being argued about or resented, but it did give them a hint that rules, as such, were more than restrictions created by an adult world to make children's lives miserable. You couldn't have a game without rules, any more than you could have a school without rules. These first impromptu games soon taught them a new word—"sport," or "good sport." You didn't cry or get mad when you struck out, dropped a fly ball, or missed a grounder. You didn't blame it on somebody else.

I remembered the time Chris had told me how he always missed the ball when he was mad. "I just can't hit it," he said. "Have to learn to control my temper."

"Then maybe you'll stop hitting your brother when you're mad," I said.

He grinned. "That's the only time I want to hit him," he said. "But I see what you mean."

The boys were finding out other things which, now that I looked back, made me feel better about this particular world they were living in. They weren't talking so loud and long about their occasional home runs or fielding feats. They were beginning to appreciate the fact that a teammate's run counted just as much as one of their own, and they were taking increasing pride in their sacrifice bunts on which others scored. The importance of teamwork was getting home to them. They were particularly happy over their increasing proficiency in executing a double play, in which they had to think and act at top speed, making sure that their performance was perfectly coordinated with that of a fellow player. They were learning to stand up under pressure, to give the best of which they were capable to the team effort.

The older they got, the harder they played, and the oftener they came home after a game with bumps and bruises, both physical and spiritual. Even as far out in the country as we lived there were few cleared areas big enough for baseball games, and those there were had an unusual number of hazards in the shapes of stones, stumps, and bushes. The cuts and minor sprains didn't bother the boys as much as the bad bounces, for it seemed bitterly unfair to them to lose a game through no fault of their own. They tried changing fields, but it didn't help much, and they gradually realized that both they and their opponents were going to get some pretty bad bounces no matter what field they played on.

They began to keep their own batting and fielding averages (to the delight of their arithmetic teachers), thereby beginning to understand that each day had its own quota of triumphs and defeats.

This thought reminded me of the morning at breakfast when Chris had been happily telling us of his good luck at bat the previous afternoon, and I had thought I'd better remind him of one of baseball's first precepts, in case he'd forgotten it.

"Just remember," I said, "that the hits you made yesterday never won today's ball game."

He was silent for a minute. "That's a good rule," he said.

I had noticed, too, a subtle change in their attitude toward winning. Of course they loved to win. But when they had played long enough to realize they couldn't win them all, or perhaps even most of them, they came to feel that being a good ballplayer implies a lot more than simply being a winning one.

Even though the boys did not wear uniforms when they played their games, now that I came to think about it I had never known them to appraise a friend in terms of his clothes, the kind of car or home his parents owned, or his race, color, or creed. The history of the game they know so well is illuminated with the names of players representing many racial and religious groups. What they want to know about a boy is what kind of ballplayer he is, and what kind of teammate.

The boys' mother and I never had to redecorate the walls of their room; they took care of that themselves with hundreds of pictures of players clipped from magazines and newspapers. One of the most prominently displayed pictures appeared the morning after the final game of the 1948 World Series. It shows Lou Boudreau, manager of the victorious Cleveland Indians, implanting a jubilant kiss on the broad cheek of Larry Doby, his Negro center fielder. The year before, Jackie Robinson, first Negro to play in the major leagues, had had a spectacularly successful first season with the Brooklyn Dodgers. Robinson and Doby helped settle one area for good and all on thousands of American playgrounds. The old cruel labels were dropped. A new boy was a potential Jackie Robinson, Phil Rizzuto, Ted Kluszewski, or Hank Greenberg.

By this time my thinking had circled back to where it had started. I shouldn't worry, I thought, about how much the boys like baseball. I should worry about how much baseball likes the boys.

->>>->>>->>)((-(((-(((-

"I see what you mean," Emily said. Then she looked at me questioningly, her eyes troubled. "But what will they use it for?" she asked. "All these wonderful reflexes, coordination, sportsmanship, and sense of team play— how will they be using them a few years from now? Throwing grenades, firing rifles, and dropping bombs?"

I walked over and sat down beside her. "Please God, no," I said, "but you could say the same thing about going to school, couldn't you? Or studying music? Or reading?"

She nodded slowly.

"We don't know what is going to be asked of the boys," I said, "but we know they can't give anything they haven't got."

After a minute she smiled. "All right," she said. "But you didn't mention the sport that statistics prove American women know more about than American men."

"What's that?" I asked.

"Driving a car," Emily said sweetly, "and we have you boys to thank for it."

"Maybe so," I said. "But why don't those statistics keep dents out of the front fenders?"

"It's got nothing to do with statistics," Emily said. "It's the garage door. It's too small."

"That's as may be," I said, "but irregardless, as we say, of the size of the garage door, you'll have to admit that sports are very important for the boys."

"I never said they weren't," Emily said, "but it is also

true that they didn't learn everything they know from sports. They have been having another experience at the same time. In case it has escaped your notice, they have also been going to school for some years now."

"Who do you think has been helping them with their homework?"

Emily gave me a long, judicial look. "About once a year you helped them," she said. Then she burst out laughing. "Remember the algebra problem you had all the fathers in the train working on one morning?"

"Well, none of them could do it either," I said. "Maybe I ought to go back to school."

"I bet I know which one you'd go to if you could," Emily said.

I had to think for only a second. Then we grinned at each other. "So do I," I said.

❧ VII ❧

WHEN WE MOVED to the country the first thing we
did was drive over to see what the boys' new
school was like. It was called Ivy Knoll, and when the
boys' mother looked at it she said, "Well, it's not the pro-
verbial little red schoolhouse that has produced so many
of America's greatest men, but it isn't far from it."

"It looks fine to me," I said. "Quiet, with trees and
country around it. The boys should have a very interesting time." This turned out to be the understatement of
the decade.

At the end of their first day they were both wrecks.

"We didn't do nothing but fight all day," Chris said.
"Me and Nicky tried to keep out of it but we couldn't."

"It is obvious that you didn't spend the day on your
grammar," I said. "What is your teacher like?"

The boys looked at each other. Then Chris said slowly,
"Well, he's kind of—ah—kind of—"

"Dopey," said Nick.

"What do you mean?" the boys' mother asked.

Little by little we got the story. Mr. Green was a small mild man faced with a group of overgrown, underdeveloped fourth-, fifth-, and sixth-graders who had quickly discovered that he could be terrorized. The day had been a chaos of threats, counter-threats, fighting, and vandalism.

"He finally had to give the two biggest boys fifty cents apiece to get them to stop," Chris said.

"I wonder how long he'll last," said the boys' mother.

After two weeks of bedlam, meetings of the school board and the PTA, Mr. Green departed a sadder if not a wiser man. We were notified that a new teacher, Mr. Barney Gill, was coming as a replacement.

"He's certainly got his work cut out for him," I said. "I wonder how he's going to make out."

Part of the answer was available at the end of the first day. On the way home from the station the boys' mother informed me that the boys had had a licking from the new teacher.

"What for?" I asked.

"I'm not quite sure," she said. "Maybe you'd better try to find out."

While the boys sat gingerly on the edges of their chairs during dinner I tried to get a play-by-play account of the fracas.

"We weren't the only ones," Chris said. "He whacked all the boys."

"What had you been doing?" I asked.

"Oh, just sort of goofing around," said Chris.

"How about Lonnie Gleeson and his pals?" I continued. Lonnie was the big six-footer who had caused the most trouble.

"Mr. Gill took Lonnie down to the basement and talked to him," Nick said. "We don't know what he said but Lonnie shut up for the whole day."

"Is he as big as Lonnie?" the boys' mother asked.

"No," said Chris, "but he's wider."

"And boy, can he spank!" said Nick, passing his hand delicately over the area of proof.

Subsequent investigation proved that Chris and Nick, along with all the other boys in the school, had been engaged in a recess adventure against which they had been specifically warned. Mr. Gill had made it quite evident that when he issued an order he expected it to be obeyed.

After they had gone to bed their mother and I discussed the matter further.

"Now that he has apparently established law and order, maybe they can get along with their lessons," I said.

The following week they came home covered with paint. Upon being questioned, they told us that Mr. Gill had discovered the washrooms to be in such a mess that the whole school had spent the day cleaning the respective washrooms and painting them. Now maybe the boys and girls would take care of the rooms, Mr. Gill had said.

"Did Annabelle Lowry look like you boys—I mean, all covered with paint?" the boys' mother asked.

"Nope," said Nick, "she just got a little bit on her dress."

"That should be enough," the boys' mother said, turning to me. "You know Mrs. Lowry."

"Well, she has something on her side," I said. "We're not sending the kids to school to learn how to paint rooms.

They're supposed to be learning how to spell and read and figure."

"I'm sure he knows what he's doing," said the boys' mother. "And remember, he made them measure all the different areas and figure out how much paint they were going to use. He made them pick colors and give reasons for the colors they chose, too. Anyway, I bet they do keep the washrooms clean after this."

"I'll look forward to their report cards," I said. "We'll see."

But we didn't see. It turned out that Mr. Gill didn't believe in report cards. He sent notes saying the boys were doing fine. They needed some of the rough edges filed off, he said, but they were coming along all right.

A little later in the year the boys reported that Mr. Gill had thrown all the desks out of his room and had made a group of square tables that could be fitted together to form one enormous table.

"Did it all himself," Chris said proudly. "Used to be a carpenter once."

"Used to be a coal miner too," Nick added.

"Anything else?" I asked.

"Sure," said Chris. "He used to work in the steel mills."

"How do you figure the area of a circle?" I asked.

"Pi r-square," said Chris, "and do you know what we're making on that great big table?"

"I can't imagine," I said.

"A typographic something of the United States," Nick said.

"That's 'topographical,' " said Chris, "and it's a map —all the mountains, rivers, everything. It's neat."

"Haven't you got anything else in the room?"I asked, feebly trying to make a joke.

"Sure," said the boys.

I was sorry I had asked. They had a working beehive, a pair of hamsters who had babies every day or so, a box of snakes, and a robin with a broken wing.

"Mr. Gill says we have to learn from the world around us as well as out of books," Chris said.

At this point I gave up. Mr. Gill was not only more than a match for the boys, he was more than a match for me. Every so often I would mention something plaintive about no report cards and how could we tell how they would do in high school when they got there, but the boys' mother was loyal to Mr. Gill.

"He's the best teacher I ever saw," she said.

During the winter he taught them square dancing at recess when the weather was too bad to play outside, and his wife wrote and directed a charming and witty children's production at the local playhouse. Several Saturdays in April and May, Mr. Gill drove out in his station wagon at five in the morning and picked up eight or ten boys and girls for bird walks.

"Isn't he wonderful?" asked the boys' mother.

"All right," I said. "I cheerfully admit he's wonderful, but I am interested in how well the boys will do in another school."

At the end of the first marking period of Chris's first year in junior high he brought home his report card. It wasn't sensational—about the middle of the class, I thought.

"How did the rest of the Ivy Knoll kids do?" I asked.

"Well, most of them better than me," Chris said. "The principal says it's the best Ivy Knoll group they ever got. And he doesn't know how Mr. Gill does it."

"Neither do I," I muttered.

The boys' mother was out shopping, and while waiting for her the boys and I got out an old set of boxing gloves. I timed the boys for several rounds and waved towels at them. Finally Chris said, "Here, you box a round with me."

I pulled on Nick's gloves, and we squared away. After a few feints I started a light left hook at the small, quick form in front of me. As I did so, Chris hit me square on the nose with as fast and accurate a straight left jab as I have ever seen.

I stepped back and sniffed. "Who in the world taught you how to do that?" I said.

"Mr. Gill," said Chris. "He used to be light heavy-weight champion of Pennsylvania."

The boys' mother went over the report card at dinner that night. She pointed out that Chris wasn't doing as well as he should. But she was delighted with the news of the rest of his class.

"See," she said, turning to me, "I was right about Mr. Gill all the time."

"You certainly were," I said. "I wish I'd kept my nose out of the whole affair."

→»»-»»-»»«««-«««-«««

"You sound pretty calm in that one," Emily said. "You weren't calm at all the night you found out that Mr. Gill had whacked the boys."

"I never objected to the boys' getting a licking. You may remember there was a time when I used to give them an occasional hit myself."

"Was a time?" Emily asked. "You mean you don't plan to any more?"

"Only if they hit me first."

"They're not likely to do that," Emily said. "Mr. Gill may have taught them something about boxing, but he taught them a lot more about birds."

"I hate to have you even mention birds," I said. "Every time you mention birds we end up with another dog."

"Only twice," Emily said.

❧ VIII ❧

OUR BOYS did not have a dog of their own until the second year we lived in the country. One night, about two weeks before Christmas, the boys' mother told me when she met me at the station that there was a surprise waiting for me at home.

When I walked into the living room I saw Chris and Nick lying on the floor playing with a small, fat black and tan cocker puppy. The three of them had identical expressions of rapture on their faces.

"He's cute," I said. "Where did we get him?"

"Some rats ate Ann Nolan's lovebirds," said the boys' mother.

"That's too bad," I said. "He sure is a fat little fellow —and look, he's really a tricolor with that white chest." Then I turned and stared at her. "What rats, and why because they ate up the lovebirds does that mean we acquire a puppy?"

It turned out to be perfectly logical. Ann and Bill Nolan supplemented their income by raising dogs and birds. The first week in December they had moved to a small farm and put the caged lovebirds in the barn. The birds had been sold and were awaiting Christmas delivery, but the first night the rats ate them all up, and Ann had had to refund the money.

"Naturally," said the boys' mother, "when we heard this we had to buy one of their puppies."

"Of course," I said. "What else?"

"It will be good for the boys," she added. "They will have something to be responsible for."

This was not the way it worked out at all. The boys named their puppy Jericho, played with him when they felt like it, but were always mysteriously missing when the dog needed attention. This attention was supplied by the boys' mother with such a marked lack of enthusiasm that she was accused of not loving the dog.

"Look," she said, "I feed the puppy, I wash him, clean up after him fifty times a day, force vitamins down him, and usually keep from stepping on him when I'm doing the housework. Do I have to love him too?"

The boys obviously interpreted this announcement to mean that she was to supply the work and they the love, so the situation remained the same. In the middle of January they took their pet to a skating party. They kept him warmly wrapped up in a blanket from one of their beds as long as they could, but on the way home they let him run along behind them. There was only one road between the pond and our house, and the boys were well across it when they remembered to look back and call to Jerry.

The driver of the car that hit him was heartbroken, as were the boys, but it was too late for anybody to do anything about it. They blamed themselves as well as the driver.

"You'd of thought he could of seen that black dog in the snow," Nick said.

"He did," Chris said wearily. "Jerry ran this way and that way. Anyway, why didn't you pick him up when we crossed the road?"

"Why didn't you?" Nick said. "He was just as much yours as mine."

The boys' mother and I discussed the advisability of getting them another puppy, but shortly after Jerry's death our attention was focused on a family of rats who came, uninvited, to live with us.

The boys connected rats with the death of the lovebirds, and somehow with Jerry's too, so they started planning a complex and grisly revenge.

"We'll chop off their heads," Chris said.

"And their tails," Nick continued.

"Then we'll dip them in gasoline and burn them," Chris concluded with a happy smile.

"Let's catch them first," said their mother.

We tried everything, starting with simple traps that went off with such a terrifying snap that the boys couldn't stand watching me set them. We baited with processed cheese. The rats spurned it. We tried store cheese. They left it alone. We tried Edam, Cheddar in port wine, and plain rat cheese. We tried bacon, salt pork, and filet mignon. Nothing tempted the rats. They lived on flour, sugar, crackers, oatmeal, and raisins. We tried poisons of all kinds. The boys' mother claimed she could hear the rats snickering at us at night.

Then I borrowed an electronic trap of marvelously intricate design.

"Don't be silly," said the boys' mother. "Any rat who can figure out how to get in there can figure his way out of it." She was right.

"If we had a dog . . ." the boys said hopefully.

"With those rats?" I said. "I wouldn't dare. Let's go find a big, rough, tough tomcat."

A neighboring farm produced a young, strong, massive, and nasty-looking yellow specimen that we brought home and christened Ramapo.

"Watch out, rats," Nick said.

Early in the evening of the day we brought Ramapo home we heard gnawing sounds from the kitchen. We shoved the cat in and closed the door. Two hours later we opened the door to view the holocaust. Ramapo was sitting on the counter beside the open breadbox, eating a jelly doughnut.

He turned out to be the sweetest and most amiable of cats. He loved the boys, he loved us, and he loved the rats. We called the exterminator.

After the exterminator pronounced us rat-free the boys took to sneering at Rampy on occasion. This obviously got under the cat's skin, because one day he showed up at the kitchen door with a large, very fierce, and very dead rat. The boys fell upon him with cries of homage and congratulation. Several days later, after the boys had stopped admiring his feat, he produced another. He got a good hand for this, but nothing like the one he had got the first time. The third time he showed up with a rat the boys were frankly suspicious.

"I think it's the same rat," Chris said.

"Where does he keep him?" Nick asked.

"Probably in somebody's icehouse," Chris said.

"Is this what got people started saying, 'I smell a rat'?" Nick asked, bending over the corpse.

We never knew how Rampy got out of it, but the fact was that the episode raised him to such a height in the boys' esteem that they asked if they could have him.

"You've already got him," the boys' mother pointed out.

"No, we mean for our own cat."

"Why, yes," said their mother. "Now let me tell you about what he eats."

They fed him conscientiously for five days. Then they decided to do it in rotation, Chris one day and Nick the next. This worked for a while, but then they started having pitched battles over whose turn it was. These led their mother to suggest that maybe they didn't love the cat.

"Not love Rampy?" they said. "We're crazy about him. Why, we love him to pieces."

"Your father and I love you to pieces too, but we manage to feed you with some regularity—and without fighting about it, either."

"That's different," Chris said.

"Oh, is it?" said his mother.

The boys did a little better after that. They remembered about Rampy's dinner most of the time, if not about his breakfast. They even gave him a bath once, which taxed Rampy's disposition to the breaking point. But somehow we didn't feel their hearts were in it.

One spring evening on the way home from the station the boys' mother said, "Oh, by the way, I got Rampy back."

"Where's he been?" I asked.

"He hasn't been any place. I mean he isn't the boys' cat any more. He's mine."

"How come?" I asked.

"Well, you know those barn swallows that built the nest in the corner of the porch?"

I nodded.

"When the eggs hatched, the boys started worrying about what would happen if one of the babies fell or got pushed out of the nest before it could fly."

"I could have told them," I said. "Rampy would eat it up."

"I know," she said. "That's what they were worrying about."

"I can't see what difference the change in the cat's ownership is going to make," I said. "Of course I'm sweet and gentle because I belong to you, but I don't think it would work with a cat. Besides, I never ate barn swallows anyway."

"Stop it," she said, "and let me finish. This afternoon they rigged a screen under the nest so that if one fell out it would fall on the screen."

"That's all right as far as it goes," I said, "but it would be just as easy for the bird to fall off the screen too."

"They know that," she said. "But they figured out that by putting up the screen they could keep the little bird's first mistake from being its last. They said they wished they'd done something like that for Jerry."

I was silent for a moment. "That's pretty good thinking," I said, "but it still doesn't explain how you got the cat back."

"The boys traded him to me."

"What for?" I asked.

She smiled at me. "A puppy," she said.

→»»-»»-»»«-««-««-«

"He's a good dog, too," Emily said, "but he's miserable when the boys go anywhere without him."

I looked down at the collie lying quietly in the corner with a mournful expression in his eyes. "Where are the boys tonight?" I asked.

"Out sitting," Emily said. "Chris is at the Barneses', and Nick is at the Arnolds'."

"Well, what do you know," I said. "Seems like only yesterday we had to get sitters for them."

"Do you miss them, dear?" Emily asked with what can only be called a sly grin.

"Miss whom—the boys?" I asked.

"No," she said. "The pretty sitters."

"Oh," I said. "Oh, we're back on that again, are we? It's about time the whole truth about that came out."

"Let it," Emily said. "I'm perfectly willing to hear your side of it."

ᥰᥴ IX ᥰᥱ

*T*HE BOYS' MOTHER did not start making cracks about pretty sitters until the summer she reached the senile age of thirty. Chris and Nick were eight and six at the time, and for some years I had been escorting attractive teen-aged girls home at various hours of the night, or occasionally, on week ends, at various hours of the morning. Apparently this routine performance never bothered her until the prospect of being thirty warped her judgment.

One night when I returned after taking the sitter home she fixed me with an accusing eye. "I don't much like the way you looked at that girl," she said.

"How did I look at her?" I asked pleasantly.

"Well, you didn't look at her as though you were seeing a nice little girl who had been taking care of your children."

"I didn't ask how I didn't look at her," I said. "I asked how I did."

"You," said the boys' mother "—you ogled her."

This seemed to me both inconsistent and silly. We had just returned from a movie that used all of Hollywood's resources to get me to ogle girls of about the same age. Furthermore, I had. I mentioned this.

"It's not the same thing," she said.

From that time on I felt as though I were living under a cloud of some kind. Nothing more was said about sitters for nearly two years; then I ran out of gas on the return trip from some young lovely's house. By the time I got the car running again I had figured out that the one thing I must not do was tell the truth. So I didn't. I told the boys' mother I had had a flat tire. I won't say she didn't believe me, but she did seem to brood about the incident.

Moving to the country simply multiplied the complications. Sitters were hard to find and they invariably lived many miles away. By far the most popular sitter the boys ever had was a girl named Sue Miller. The real secret of her success was unknown to us until after her marriage, when she reported that she used to tell the boys they could do anything they wanted, provided they had the house cleaned up and were in bed one half-hour before we were expected home. This rule apparently had led to a series of engagements that made the Battle of Stalingrad seem like a tea party. Pillow fights were the first course; from there they progressed to maneuvers with water pistols. This usually led to bombing engagements with bags full of water. From then on in, they improvised. It is a credit to their cleaning abilities that we never suspected anything at the time.

We were deprived of Sue's services by a most unlikely

incident. Her home was four miles down the road from our house, and one summer day when we were going out for the afternoon and an early supper, she announced that she need not be fetched as she was going to ride her bike up. We waited and waited and waited. Finally we called her home, and there was no answer. We regretfully canceled our date and waited some more. Late in the afternoon Sue's mother called up. Sue had left for our house in plenty of time but had come home some minutes later, shaken and bleeding from a small gash in her ankle. A dog had attacked her, thrown her off her bicycle, and bitten her.

She was so upset, her mother said, that she couldn't remember whose dog it had been or what the dog had looked like. So Mrs. Miller had taken Sue in her car and started up the road. At every house where there was a known dog they would stop. "Is that the dog that bit you?" Mrs. Miller would ask.

Sue would look at the dog tearfully and say no, that was not the dog. Finally they got to the Wilsons' house. Mrs. Wilson was in the garden, and her great Dane, Blue, was lying beside her in the shade of the arbor vitae. Mrs. Miller and Sue approached, and Sue was asked the question. She looked at Blue carefully and said no, that was not the dog that had bitten her. Whereupon Blue got up, came over, and bit her.

Mrs. Miller said that neither bite was serious but Sue was in no condition to sit.

When the boys were twelve and ten we were still paying sitters. I thought they were old enough to sit rather than be sat with.

"It's high time they got in on this baby-sitting racket," I said. But this kind of remark got me nowhere, and time went by—or I should say time-and-a-half went by, because the rates kept going up.

Then the news got around that we didn't have television, and the problem of sitters became acute. Just when it became impossible, the situation resolved itself in a most unpredictable manner.

As it turned out, the last sitter we ever had was the prettiest. When we got home from our party the boys' mother took one admiring look at her and said, "It's such a lovely night and the moonlight is so beautiful that I think I'll just go along for the ride."

When we pulled up in front of the sitter's house, I opened the car door and let her out. "Walk up to the porch with her," the boys' mother whispered. "What will her parents think?"

On the way home I suddenly turned into a side road and parked in the shadow of some tall poplars. "What are you stopping for?" she asked warily.

"To neck," I said. "That's what I always do on these trips. Don't you remember?"

"Why, you've developed a taste for older women," she said fondly. "How nice."

"Just because you have two gigantic boys doesn't mean you are an older woman," I said. "Don't forget you were a child bride." I lunged at her.

She evaded me. "You are a nice man," she said, "but you are mad with moonlight, and besides, that was as halfhearted a pounce as you ever pounced."

"Oh, it was, was it?" I muttered, preparing to strike again.

She cowered in the corner. "We've really got to get home," she said. "I'm worried about the boys."

As I said, that was the last sitter we ever had. The next development involved some complicated chicanery in which we paid the boys for sitting with themselves.

Finally the time came when our friends would pay the boys more for sitting with their children than we paid them for sitting with themselves. Of course the poor underprivileged, televisionless fellows would have paid *them* to spend the evening in a fully equipped home, but I would have been a fool to bring that up.

This more or less brings us up to the time when two of the prettiest teen-aged girls you ever saw spent the evening at our house. I drove them home a little after midnight—through the moonlight, too. The boys' mother, mellowing somewhat at the prospect of being forty, did not insist upon going along for the ride this time. But the boys did.

-»»-»»-»»-«««-«««-«««-

"I don't see why you had to put in that part about my being forty," Emily said.

"I didn't say you were forty. I said you were approaching forty. As far as that goes, you have been approaching forty ever since you were born."

She smiled. "Looks as if I'm going to make it any day now, doesn't it?"

"You don't have to be forty if you don't want to," I said. "You can be thirty-nine as long as you like."

She thanked me for the license. "Do you remember what happened to Nick that first night he sat with Polly Arnold?"

"Not quite," I said.

"She was a strenuous child," Emily said. "Nick played so many games with her that he was exhausted. Then he kept putting her to bed, and she kept getting up, and finally he got so tired that he went to sleep on the couch, and when the Arnolds got home Polly was sitting up with him."

"And girls have been running both the boys ragged ever since," I said.

"Not only the boys—you too," said Emily.

"I don't know what you mean."

"Don't tell me you've forgotten the night you were going to murder the whole gang for making so much noise when you wanted to read?"

I hadn't.

❧ X ❧

B Y THE TIME Chris was sixteen and his brother Nick
fourteen they had arrived at the conclusion that if
a thing was worth doing it was worth doing quickly. This
belief usually plunged the family into chaos. Once they
decided on a Thursday to have some of their friends for
dinner and the evening on Friday.

"Just about eight, that's all," Chris said. He counted
off the names.

"You forgot Edith," Nick said.

"If we ask Edith we'll have to ask Edwin, that goony
brother of hers," Chris said.

"I have already asked Edith," said Nick.

By the time the guest list had been settled, screened,
and resettled, there were to be twelve for dinner. Now
for the menu.

"Steak and french fries," said the boys.

"Do you mind if I grind it first?" the boys' mother
asked. "And what for a vegetable?"

"Do we have to have a vegetable? At a party?"

A compromise was reached at carrot-and-raisin salad. For the dessert they ordered ice cream and cake.

It was further stipulated that, though their mother would be glad to prepare the dinner, the boys would have to serve and clean up afterward.

"Do the dishes right after dinner?" they exclaimed. "Holy smoke, we'd never get to our own party."

"We do the dishes after our parties," said the boys' mother firmly. "You do them after yours."

"But you don't do them till the next morning," Nick said with uncomfortable accuracy. Further arbitration produced a schedule that called for the dishes to be scraped and stacked after dinner and washed the following morning.

At this point they reached for the football, but their mother had other matters to discuss. "Now, about your room."

"What about our room?" they asked with one voice.

"It will have to be cleaned up. Your guests will have to put their coats and hats there, and you don't want your friends to see your room looking the way it does now, do you?"

"But it always looks like that."

"That," said the boys' mother, "is exactly the point."

They came home right after school on Friday and cleaned the room. This took longer than they had anticipated, because they found several things that had been missing and needed playing with. For once they took baths without threat of deportation, and while their mother made enough hamburgers and french fries for a regiment I made the salad. The boys' mother told me I hadn't made enough; not being much of a salad man myself, I figured I had made too much.

"What are we going to do for dinner?" I asked her.

I was told that a dainty supper for two would be served in our room.

"Have the boys figured out what they are going to do for entertainment?"

"I asked that," said their mother. "Chris said they were going to play records and dance."

At six-thirty all the guests arrived at once. I stayed around just long enough to meet them. Then I went back to the bedroom and, sure enough, there was a card table set for dinner for two. With candles. And a bottle of wine.

I waited for about half an hour, and finally the boys' mother came with a platter over which was thrown a large napkin.

"I had to smuggle this over the border," she said. Underneath the napkin was a steak. There were also french-fried potatoes and a mound of carrot-and-raisin salad.

The boys' mother ate too fast. "Quit gulping your food," I said. "What's your hurry?"

"I have to get back out to the kitchen," she said, "to help serve the dessert."

She finished her dinner and left. I waited. After she had been gone long enough both to make the ice cream and to serve it, I went out and looked in the dining-room door. She had pulled a chair up to the table and was sitting between two of the girls, explaining how to knit cable-stitch socks. I listened, fascinated. I had never known she could do it. Finally I beckoned to her.

When she got to the living room I said, "What do you mean, horning in on their party? Don't you remember how bored we got when they used to hang around our parties? And incidentally, for whom have you been knitting those fancy socks?"

"I just finished one for my father," she said. "Come on, we'll go back to the bedroom." We finished the wine, and the boys' mother yawned.

"Will you take the dishes out?" she said. "I think I'll go to bed and read for a while."

"Do I have to scrape them?" I asked.

She didn't honor me with an answer, but I scraped them anyway, adding them to the sink that was already full. On my way back through the living room I heard Chris explaining some of the flight characteristics of the old P-40 fighter. I cleared up a couple of points for him, and then we got into a discussion of the theory of the gull-wing Stuka. I believe I was telling the group about how the Fifth Infantry Division took Frankfurt when I heard a "Pssssst!" from the doorway. The boys' mother was summoning me.

"Why don't you leave them alone?" she said. "They can't have any fun while you're around."

"I am not so sure about that," I said. "They're nice kids, and they were interested."

"In the fall of Frankfurt?" she said. "I doubt it. That's ancient history."

"Not to me it isn't," I said. "All right, I'll leave them alone." I took off my coat and tie and put my slippers on. The boys' mother, in her red challis housecoat, lay on the bed, reading *Mansfield Park*. I got the paperback edition of *Three Deaths to the Wind* and sat down to read in the chintzy bedroom chair that is more comfortable than a sawhorse but not much more.

Then the music started. It started with screaming brasses, piercing clarinets, and pounding basses and drums. The bedroom door quivered visibly. So did I.

"Do they have to turn it up that high?" I said.

The boys' mother turned a page. "Yes," she said.

"But they can't hear themselves talk."

"They're not talking," she said. "They're dancing. And besides, don't you know enough about teen-age parties to know that you don't worry when there's too much noise, you worry when there's too little?"

"Why?" I asked, my mind on Inspector Cartwright.

She didn't answer, and after a while I looked up. She had closed the book and was staring at me with a most peculiar expression.

"Oh," I said. "Oh, sure, but aren't they a little young for that?"

"Were you?" she asked, picking up the book again. I rejoined Inspector Cartwright without answering.

Five minutes later she said, "Neither was I."

The music got louder. Now they were playing a section of something that was all drums—big drums, little drums, medium-sized drums. The floorboards picked up the beat.

"That is enough," I announced. "There's a limit to human endurance. Surely it's not too much to ask them to keep it as quiet around here as the White Sands Proving Grounds."

I flung the book in the corner and started for the door.

I was stopped by the sound of giggling from the bed. The boys' mother never giggles.

"What's the matter with you?" I asked.

She finally got control of herself. "Don't you recognize it?" she gasped.

"I never heard it before. That's bebop or something —I don't know."

"It is not. Don't you remember Jackson Heights in nineteen-forty-one? That's Artie Shaw's 'Concerto for Clarinet.'" She started giggling again. "You brought it home. You loved it. You played it every night for weeks." She stuffed a corner of the pillowcase into her mouth. "You played it with the volume turned way up." Tears came to her eyes. She rolled back and forth. "The bass turned up so you could hear the drums, and the treble turned up so you could hear the c-c-c-c-c-clarinet."

"There, there," I said, sitting down beside her. "Don't take on so. As a matter of fact, it does sound vaguely familiar."

She was still shaking with laughter. "You kept them awake night after night with it, and now they—" She could no longer talk.

I brought her the box of Kleenex. She wiped her eyes. "You ought to be glad they like our old records," she said. "Think of how much money it saves."

The whole thing did begin to seem funny to me. "The music goes round and round," I said, "and now it comes out here in our bedroom."

After that they played some of the wonderful Goodman sextets, then some Dixieland. When "Begin the Beguine" started I got up, went over, and stood beside the bed. The boys' mother was smiling at me.

"Shall we dance, madam?" I said, bowing slightly from what I still refer to as my waist.

She closed her book. "I think that is a lovely idea, sir," she said. So we did.

→»→»→»«←«←«←

"My, I had a good time that night," Emily said. "When are you going to dance with me again?"

"I had a good time too. I bet we had more fun than the boys. And when the boys are in college we'll go dancing every night."

"You're just saying that," Emily said. "I'd settle for twice a year.

"It's going to seem funny not having them living at home," she continued. "When I think of all the things we've done together . . ."

"Well, that won't suddenly stop," I said. "We'll have vacations and summers."

"Not the way we used to have," she said. "In vacations they'll be interested in girls and parties, and in the summers they'll have to work to help out with college."

"Come now," I said. "We'll do lots of things. We'll take trips, maybe go camping, or fishing."

"Not fishing," said Emily. "They'll never want me to go fishing with them again."

"Why, the one you went on was a fine one," I said. "I can't imagine what you're worrying about."

❧ XI ❧

CHRIS AND NICK planned the whole thing themselves. "We'll get up early, see," they said, "and drive up to High Meadow Lake and catch a big mess of bass and have a breakfast feast right there on the shore." The boys' mother said she'd like to go, and we welcomed her.

The night before the expedition the boys were talking about equipment. "Just a frying pan," Chris said. "Like in the Old West, we'll live off the land."

"Well, you'll need a few more things," said the boys' mother. "I don't think it would be much fun to eat fish with your fingers." Somewhat reluctantly the boys agreed to forks and plates.

"Then you'd better take a little grease to fry the fish in." That was an obvious necessity.

"I am not averse to a cup of coffee in the morning, either," she added. The boys were good sports about the coffee, but you could see that they felt such domestic trappings were not in the true spirit of the thing.

After supper we went out and collected some night

crawlers for bait. We would stop at a small pond on the
way up in the morning and net some minnows, whic⁻
were better for catching bass.

The morning was fine and clear, and the boys spurned
offers of cereal and milk. "You don't seem to get the
pitch," Nick said. "We are going to catch our breakfast.
That's the whole idea."

I must confess I looked a little wistfully at the fresh
brown eggs in the icebox, but it was obvious that I had
to stick with the men. "Okay, boys," I said. "I'll string
along with you. You be the big providers this morning."

"Are you going to eat all the fish you catch?" the boys'
mother asked.

"Sure, why?" Chris asked.

"Well," she said, "I thought I'd take some darning
along to do, and if you're not going to need the fishing
creel I thought I'd use it for some socks and things."

The boys agreed, and we waited in the car while their
mother packed the wicker basket creel with what she
needed.

"Women certainly take a lot of stuff when they go
some place, don't they?" Chris said indulgently. I agreed.

"I like to travel light," Nick said.

The sun was just up over the hills, and it was cool as
we started up the steep mountain road. We stopped at
the minnow pond and with a few scoops of the net we
caught all the minnows we would need. We put them
in a pailful of water on the floor of the back seat. It
sloshed a little when we hit bumps.

The road to the lake branched off from the main road,
and the last four miles were steep and rocky. Trees

arched over the road, and grass grew thickly between the ruts. About halfway up, Nick saw a mammoth pileated woodpecker, and farther on we stopped to watch a doe and fawn feeding peacefully in a clearing.

We parked the car by the shore of the lake. The boys baited their hooks and started fishing. I arranged some stones to make a fireplace, and collected wood. The boys' mother sat down with the creel in her lap, leaned back against a smooth boulder, and began darning socks. She was humming "The Happy Wanderer."

A half-hour later we hadn't even had a bite.

"Let's try worms," said Chris.

"You won't get a bass with worms," Nick said, "but bluegills are pretty good eating." The boys changed bait, but I kept on with a minnow. I was going to have bass for breakfast or nothing.

After another half-hour it looked like nothing.

"Why don't you light the fire and make some coffee?" the boys' mother said. This was obviously better than nothing, so I boiled some water and measured the coffee into it. I waited for some remark from her about camp coffee, but all she said was how good it was.

Nick decided to try his luck in another spot. As he was walking down the shore the tip of his rod caught at an angle in the crotch of a branch. He pulled at it angrily. The tip broke off. He came back to us with his lips pressed tight together.

"That ends my fishing," he said.

I examined the break. "We might be able to fix it," I said, "if we had some strong thread to wind it with."

The boys' mother put down her darning cotton and reached into the creel. "Like this?" she asked.

Nick's face lightened. "Just like that," he said.

We wound the break carefully and strongly. "We really should have some shellac to fix it properly," I said, "but I guess it will do."

"What about some of this red nail enamel?" the boys' mother suggested.

It looked funny, but it did a wonderful job. We drank some more coffee, and I kept putting wood on the fire. Grease was sputtering in the skillet. Everything was ready for breakfast, but the only fish we had were the minnows we had brought with us. They were looking bigger all the time.

Suddenly Chris yelled, "I got one, I got one!" His rod was bent double. "A whopper," he rejoiced.

Nick's voice sounded. "Me too, me too." His rod was an arc.

"Hurray," I said. "We eat."

Both the boys' rods went slack at the same time. They reeled in their lines sadly. The news was worse than they had imagined. They had apparently hooked into a log or a stump under water, and in pulling too hard they had broken their leaders. Their hooks were gone.

"Did you bring extra hooks, Nick?" Chris asked.

"No," said Nick. "I thought you were going to."

They looked at each other, and then they looked at us. Three or four years ago there would have been tears, but they were too big for that now.

The boys' mother reached into the creel. "I've got some pretty big pins in here," she said. "Seems to me I can remember when boys fished all the time with bent pins."

It took us fifteen minutes to get the pins bent into shape. They didn't have barbs, but a careful fisherman could make out all right.

The boys baited up and went back to work. They were grim now. They had contracted to feed us, and they didn't want to fall down on the job. They tried new places along the shore. They even waded in up to their knees to get to advantageous locations.

There wasn't a sign of a fish.

After another half-hour the boys' mother said, "I'm hungry."

We treated this remark with the silent scorn it deserved. She shrugged her shoulders. "Of course," she said, "none of you mighty fishermen thought to ask me whether I *liked* fish for breakfast."

We looked at her stonily.

"As a matter of fact," she went on, "I don't like fish for breakfast. What I like for breakfast is bacon and eggs." Failing to get any response from us, she continued, "So I brought some."

"You what?" we asked in unison.

"I brought some," she said calmly. "Would one of you cook for me, or is the age of chivalry dead?"

"I'll cook," I said.

She reached into the creel and brought out a fresh brown egg. It was one of the ones I had yearned after in the icebox. Then she took out another. And another. Finally there were eight brown eggs lying in the sun beside her. Her hand came out of the creel again, holding a pound of sliced bacon. Another trip produced half a loaf of bread. The corners of the boys' mouths were turning up for the first time in hours.

"You," I said, "sitting there with that smirk on your face, never ate that much breakfast in your life."

"How did I know how hungry I was going to get?" she said.

"How hungry are you?" Chris asked.

"Not very," she said. "I doubt whether I could eat more than two eggs and a couple of pieces of bacon."

We fried the bacon crisp and cooked the eggs in the deep fragrant fat. We made toast over the coals. It was a wonderful breakfast.

The boys had left their lines in the water, the butts of the rods secured by stones, and just as we were getting ready to go we heard the zing of the reels. The boys scrambled over to the rods, and in a few minutes each had landed a small-mouth black bass. The fish were beauties, both over two pounds.

The boys looked around for something to wrap them in for the trip home.

Their mother opened the creel. "If you'll put on these dry socks instead of the wet ones you have on now," she said, "you can use the creel. It's empty."

She looked down at the big bass. "I'll cook them as soon as we get home," she said. "I love fish for lunch."

>>>->>>->>>>-<<<-<<<-<<<

"That's what I mean," Emily said. "I sound more like a mother in a book than I do like me."

"Well, that's what happened," I said.

"I know it's what happened," Emily said in a discouraged voice, "but I wish I hadn't happened to have so many indispensable things with me that morning."

"Cheer up," I said, "there were times when you didn't."

"I know there were," she said, "but you don't write about those."

"In a short book," I said, "there isn't room for everything."

"I know there isn't," Emily said. "And now that we're talking about the book, I notice that so far all the pieces have been written from your standpoint. Why don't you try one from mine?"

"Writing from your standpoint would make it fiction," I said, "and this book is supposed to be non-fiction."

"I don't see why it would have to be fiction," Emily said. "You know what I am thinking lots of times when I don't tell you."

"That I do," I said. "Even when you are giving out nothing but waves of static the communication is remarkably good."

"Static?" she asked, raising her eyebrows.

I didn't answer. I just grinned at her.

"Oh," she said, "you mean times like that."

"Just so. Times like that."

"It's all part of the record," Emily said primly. "It ought to be in there."

"I'll do it," I said, "but on one condition."

"What's the condition?"

"That you don't change a word of it."

"It'll be hard," Emily said, "but I'll try."

◄§ XII §►

THE BOYS' MOTHER had had a bad day. It had started when I not only left the cap off the toothpaste but dropped the tube on the floor and stepped on it. My morning schedule does not give me time enough to deal with emergencies like this, and I had eaten breakfast and was halfway to New York before the thought occurred to me that it might have been nice if I had warned her about it.

As the day progressed it turned out that the toothpaste was the least of her worries.

The weather was cool and pleasant for July, and she decided it was an ideal opportunity both to get the back yard cleaned up and to replenish the boys' funds by paying them to do the job.

They weren't in the mood for it.

"The car is disgracefully dirty," she said. "How about that?"

They were not in the mood for that either and retired to their room to play the radio and decide exactly what it was they were in the mood for.

The boys' mother went to the kitchen to do the dishes. The window over the sink overlooks the back yard as completely as the boys had overlooked doing anything about it, so by the time the dishes were done she was in a great frame of mind.

Then the dishwater wouldn't run out.

She looked for the plumber's snake but couldn't find it. Finally she asked the boys.

They considered the question. "Could that have been that wire thing we used to hold up the corner of our tree house?" Nick asked Chris.

Chris nodded, and their mother left them—silently, she assures me. She had marketing to do and went to the bathroom to clean up. That was when she slipped on the toothpaste. When she got into the car and pushed the starter button nothing happened. The battery was dead.

It developed that Chris had been practicing parking the evening before and had neglected to turn off the ignition.

"The least you can do now," said the boys' mother, "is to wash it after you take the battery up to the garage to be charged." With this instruction she went to take the local bus to town. While she was picking up supplies, she told me later, she began to think that she had been kind of cross with the boys, so she got them some ice cream for lunch.

On the way back the bus had a puncture, and while she waited the ice cream melted and ran out the bottom of the bag over her clean skirt.

"Naturally," she said, "it was the boys' fault."

After lunch she suggested that if she could enjoy a short respite from dishwashing the agents who were responsible would not go unrewarded.

"Yesterday," countered the boys, "we mowed the lawn."

"You mowed part of the lawn," she pointed out. "What you left was the hard part and the clipping. This place is beginning to look like a poor man's *Tobacco Road*. Nobody has done any work outside for weeks. And you two are not the only ones I have plans for. I've got something in mind for your father too."

Just at this moment, with the outcome of the day trembling in the balance, the Model A Ford drove past the house. This car is remarkable because it is the only car our collie chases. So away went the dog, and away went the boys to recover him. That was the last sight she had of boys and dog for the rest of the afternoon.

While the boys' mother was washing the kitchen floor, after having drained the dishwater out through the trap, a shiny new car drove up, and an immaculate and fastidious lady of our acquaintance came in for a visit.

It was evident that she had not been expected. "But didn't your husband give you the message?" she asked. "I called him in New York yesterday."

The boys got home right after she had left. Where had they been? their mother asked.

Their story showed marked creative ability. The collie, it seemed, had finally been found watching an informal baseball game. The game didn't need the dog, but it did need the boys.

"We couldn't let all those fellows down," they explained. "We more or less had to stay to fill out the teams."

"I take it you don't mind letting me down," their mother said grimly. "Go get the battery; as soon as your father gets home we'll start putting new screening in those doors."

At the appointed time she drove the four miles to the station to meet me. The train was late, and the soufflé for the early supper was in the oven. She tried to call the boys, but our line was busy. When the train finally came in I wasn't on it. When she got home Chris was still on the phone with his girl, and the soufflé was a crisp memory.

After a dinner of scrambled eggs and chopped spinach, which the boys ate with the manners of reluctant martyrs, they vanished again, this time in the direction of the back yard. Their dog lay mournfully beside his empty dish.

"Can't you even feed your dog?" the boys' mother shouted out the back window into an unresponsive void.

At eight-thirty I showed up in a taxi. "I'm sorry," I said. "I was held up at the office."

"You might have called," she said, slamming the remains of the soufflé down on the kitchen counter.

"I tried several times," I said, "but the line was busy or didn't answer, and I had other things to do."

"Meaning that I have nothing to do except sit beside the phone?"

"My, my," I said, "we are in a jolly mood, aren't we?"

Chris came in and asked where the hammer was.

"I don't know," his mother answered. "Am I supposed

to keep track of every item in the whole house?" She looked at him inquiringly. "And what do you need the hammer for anyway? I thought you were going out there to do some weeding."

"Oh, we're not weeding," Chris said. "Me and Nicky are fixing the basketball hoop." He found the hammer in the salad bowl where he had left it.

"All day they goofed," said the boys' mother in a shaky voice. "There were things I wanted them to do, and I thought when you got home we could have an early supper and finish fixing the screen doors. Everything's gone wrong."

"It was no picnic in New York," I said, opening the icebox door. "Aren't there any lemons left?"

"The boys used them all up this morning."

"Why can't they use that concentrated lemon mix?" I said. "There's lots of that."

"They like fresh lemons better," she said. "It makes more mess when they squeeze them."

"I like fresh lemons too."

"Well, maybe if you got home earlier—"

I slammed the icebox door. There was a breaking noise from inside. The boys' mother looked at me with wide, angry eyes. Her lower lip was trembling. The telephone rang.

"Let it ring," I said. She turned away.

The phone rang with growing insistence for some time. Finally the outside door opened and I heard Chris muttering, "Why doesn't somebody answer the phone?"

We couldn't hear what he said on the phone because Nicky pounded through the kitchen door, waving a bleeding thumb. He explained what had happened in a few colorful phrases.

"I haven't washed your mouth out with soap for a long time," I said, "but that doesn't mean I couldn't do it."

His mother rinsed the thumb with cold water. "Get the Band-Aid box," she ordered. "It's there on the shelf with the herbs, next to the orégano."

Chris was standing in the door to the dining room, looking at us with a most peculiar expression. At first I thought he was about to burst out crying. Then I realized it was laughter that he was stifling.

"Who was that on the phone?" the boys' mother asked, pressing the Band-Aid into place.

"It was Mrs. Pearce from the playhouse," he said. "She says for me to tell you that they have been waiting for you for over half an hour."

His mother started to say something, then clapped her hand over her mouth. "I forgot," she wailed. "I'm supposed to be helping them with the new set. I've got all the paint and brushes they have to use."

There was silence. Nick looked at us in turn. "Everybody goofed," he said cheerfully.

That did it. We broke down in helpless laughter, pointing shaking fingers of accusation at one another. When quiet was restored, the boys' mother said, "I'd better get changed and hurry over there."

"I'll make a sandwich and come with you," I said. "Probably they can use an extra hand."

"Let's all go," Chris said. "Maybe it'll change our luck."

"Okay," I said. "Chris, you make me a sandwich. Nick, you put the paint and brushes in the car and feed the dog, and I'll get out of my store clothes."

By the time the boys' mother was ready we were all in the car. The collie and I were still chewing. She slid into the seat beside me, turned, and looked around. "Got everything?" she asked.

"I doubt it," I said, "but I bet we can make out with what we have."

She looked at me for a minute and said, "I guess we can."

→»→»→»«←«←«←

Emily shook her head. "My, what a day that was. There weren't many as bad as that, though."

"I should hope not," I said. "And you always got over your mad spells pretty quickly."

"It's nice of you to say so," she said. "You almost always mended the things you broke when you were mad, too."

"Thanks," I said. "And by the way, do you remember what I broke in the icebox that day?"

"Nothing but a glass icebox dish," she said. "It shouldn't have been that far out on the shelf anyway." She was silent for a while, smiling a little.

"What are you thinking about?" I asked.

"Oh," she said, "I was just thinking back and remembering how much goes into the making of a family instead of—you know, two adults and some children."

"I can remember when we didn't know much about it, too," I said.

"And I can remember," Emily said, "when the boys taught us a lesson in it."

"I guess they've taught us a lot," I said. "Have you got something special in mind?"

She had.

⊰ XIII ⊱

ABOUT HALFWAY through breakfast one Saturday morning I asked where Chris was.

"Still in bed," said the boys' mother. "He doesn't feel well."

"On a Saturday morning in June?" I asked. "What's the matter with him?"

She said she didn't know.

"And the Panthers have a game this afternoon," Nick said.

"Has he got a temperature?" I asked. This question started one of the "where-is-it" games that our family plays with infuriating regularity. The thermometer was finally located in Nick's pencil box, imitating a fountain pen.

Chris was lying in bed, listening to the radio. His face was flushed and his eyes were bright. His forehead felt pretty hot.

"Where do you hurt?" I asked.

He gestured down over his body. "All over, kind of," he said. I put the thermometer in his mouth.

The boys' mother was standing beside me. "They're not much better at telling where they hurt than when they were little," she said.

"I don't know," I said. "Maybe he does hurt all over." The thermometer read over one hundred and one.

"It feels something like a stomach ache," Chris said.

"Shall I get the pan?" his mother asked.

"I don't think it's that kind of a stomach ache," Chris said. We gave him some aspirin and went into the living room.

"Any polio around?" I asked.

The boys' mother looked at me, biting her lip. "I haven't heard of any," she said.

Nick came in from the kitchen. "How is Chris?" he asked.

"We don't know," I said. "He's got a fever and he hurts."

"Why don't you call the doctor?" Nick suggested.

"That's an interesting idea," I said. "Why don't we?"

Dr. Josephy was not immediately available, but his wife told us she could get a message to him and he would be along as soon as he could. In the next couple of hours Chris's spirits went down and his temperature went up. Toast and tea went untouched beside his bed, but he liked the alcohol rub I gave him.

His mother began to fidget. "Why doesn't the doctor come?" she said. "He's had plenty of time to get here."

"He'll get here," I said. But I called again to make sure. He was on his way.

When I went out to the kitchen the boys' mother had

set up the ironing board and was ironing jeans furiously. As far as I knew, they were the first jeans to get ironed in our house for years.

"I had to iron something," she explained.

A little while later the doctor came. He examined Chris carefully. He tapped him and felt him and tested him. He moved all his joints and peered down his throat and up his nose. Then he put his tools back in his bag and closed it with a snap.

"I'm going to send this boy to the hospital for a blood count," he said. "I want Mosconi to look at him too."

We went into the living room, and he called the hospital.

"What do you think it is?" the boys' mother asked.

"There's something in a lower quadrant that I don't like," he said, "but I can tell better after a blood count."

We walked out to his car with him. "It's appendicitis, isn't it?" asked the boys' mother.

"I think so," said Dr. Josephy. "If it is, we'll find out quick enough." He started the car. "Don't worry," he said. "He'll be all right."

"'Don't worry,'" she said as he drove away. "That's all he can say—'Don't worry.' Just have Chris at the hospital in an hour and don't worry."

I took her arm and we started into the house. "We haven't got much time," I said.

"What are we going to tell Chris?" his mother asked me.

"What do you mean?"

"There are whole books written about preparing your

child for his first trip to the hospital. And we've never done anything about it at all."

"You get changed," I said. "I'll see what I can do."

Chris was lying on his back, looking up at the ceiling. The radio was turned up loud, and his face had lost some of its flush.

"What's the matter with my quadrant?" he asked.

"That's not a thing," I said, "that's a place, and we're going to take you over to the hospital and have another doctor look at you."

He got out of bed without a word. He had trouble moving, and I helped him into the freshly pressed jeans and a T shirt.

"How old were you when you first went to a hospital?" he asked.

"Couple of years younger than you," I said. "About twelve."

"What did they do to you?" he asked.

"Oh, took out my appendix," I said.

"Maybe that's what they'll do to me."

"Maybe it is," I said, "but don't worry. It's a great hospital, and they'll have you fixed up in no time."

"They've probably got better anesthetics now than when you went," Chris said.

"Nobody said you were going to need an anesthetic," I said. "Maybe they'll just keep you overnight and send you right home."

"I kind of hope it is my appendix," Chris said. "Then it would be over with and it wouldn't happen on a hiking trip or some place."

The boys' mother came in. She was wearing the skirt

to one suit and the jacket to another. Her lipstick was on a little crooked. She put her arms around Chris.

"How are you, dear?" she asked.

"All right," he said. "How are you?"

She sighed and got a small suitcase out of the closet. "Let's see, you'll need pajamas, and a toothbrush, and some other things." She looked quickly around the room. "I think there are some clean pajamas in the basket. I'll go see." I went with her.

Nick was on the phone. "We'll have to get another pitcher," he was saying. "Chris won't be able to make it."

When we got back to the boys' room Chris had closed the bag. "I found the pajamas," he said. "I think I've got everything."

His mother carried the bag, and I put my arm around him. We asked Nick whether he wanted to go with us, and he said he guessed he didn't. "I've got some more guys to call up, so I'll stay here," he said.

I put my hand in my pocket. "I'll give you lunch money," I said. "You can go up to the stand and get some hamburgers and french fries."

"Never mind," he said. "I got money." He turned to Chris. "If it's your appendix maybe you can bring it back in a bottle."

"Sure," Chris said. "We'll put it on our mantelpiece with the model airplanes."

By this time I had had my hand in all my pockets. "Where's the key to the car?" I said. "I had it right here a minute ago."

"I saw it somewhere," said the boys' mother. I looked

in the bedroom and the bathroom. She looked in the kitchen and the dining room. Chris stood in the middle of the living room with his hands on the back of a chair.

"Why don't you use the spare key?" he asked. "The one that's hanging on a nail over the icebox."

On the way to the hospital the boys' mother said suddenly, "I forgot, you should have brought your bathrobe and slippers."

"I did," Chris said.

I had considerable trouble delivering the patient to the proper entrance of the hospital, possibly because I came in over a driveway marked EXIT.

Chris was settled in a semi-private room with a garage mechanic whose leg was in traction, and I went to the cashier's window to supply needed information. This routine was not speeded up by the fact that I had forgotten to bring my wallet, which contained our hospitalization certificate.

We sat and waited for the results of the examination.

"At the worst it's appendicitis, isn't it," the boys' mother told me.

"What it probably is," I said, "is a gigantic belly ache. The Lord only knows what those boys eat."

We were sitting in silence when Dr. Josephy came out. He sat down beside us. "It's a fine case of acute appendicitis," he said. "I thought it was. That's why I asked you to bring him right over here. But it seems to be a little out of place, and I wanted to be sure before I said anything."

"When are you going to operate?" asked the boys' mother.

"Right away. Dr. Mosconi is getting ready now."

We went in to see Chris. They had given him a pill, and he was already getting drowsy.

"Remember to tell them to put it in a bottle for me," he said.

"It's nothing," said the mechanic. "You'll be out of here long before I will."

When they came to take him to the operating room we went back to the waiting room. The boys' mother went to the phone to call Nick.

"All the Panthers were there," she said when she came back. "They sent their regards to Chris."

It seemed to us that the operation took an interminable amount of time. The boys' mother got a lapful of movie magazines, and I picked out an imposing volume from an oak bookcase with glass doors that lifted up and slid back. All I remember about the book is that it was heavy.

Finally Dr. Mosconi came down to us. He pulled off his mask and grinned. "No trouble at all," he said. "You can have him back in four or five days. He won't be doing any pitching for a while, though."

We went to the corridor and watched them wheel Chris to his room. His body looked very slight under the sheet, and he had no color at all.

After we had thanked the doctors we decided to drive home for a while and come back later.

"Well," said the boys' mother as we drove out the hospital driveway, "one appendix down and one to go. I wonder how Nicky made out today."

"I'm anxious to find out," I said. "He's probably about to come apart."

When we walked in the front door of the house there was something singular about the hall. It was picked up and vacuumed. The living room, too, was orderly and clean. Usually by suppertime on week ends the house looks as if a rodeo had been held in it.

"Where are the Panther tracks?" the boys' mother asked.

Nick was in the kitchen. He shut the oven door quickly when we came in. "How's Chris?" he asked.

"Everything's fine," said his mother. "Did you do all the cleaning up?"

"Sure," said Nick. "After the Panthers left and before the Dawsons came."

"The Dawsons?" the boys' mother asked.

"Yeah," said Nick, "and some aunt. You asked them for cocktails."

"Oh, my Lord," she said. "We forgot all about it. What did you do?"

Nick scratched his head. "Well, I told them about Chris, and then I asked them to sit down and have a drink."

"What did you give them?" I asked.

"Martinis," Nick said. "And I mixed them right too —eight to one. See, I remembered."

"Eight to one what?" I said.

"Eight little glasses of ver-mowth and one glass of gin." He smiled knowingly. "The prices were still on the bottles, and I used the most of what was cheaper."

"How did they like them?" I asked.

"They said they were great," Nick said. "They just weren't very thirsty." He walked over to the icebox. "There's quite a lot left if you want some. I put it in here."

"It's just exactly what we want," the boys' mother said. She pointed toward the oven. "What have you got in there?"

"I found a box of that cake mix," Nick said, "so I made a cake. But it didn't turn out very well."

His mother put her arm around him. "Never mind," she said. "It's the only thing that didn't."

→≫-≫-≫ ≪-≪-≪

"We've been awfully lucky in not having anything really bad happen to the boys," Emily said.

"We certainly have," I said. *"Or trouble, either. I mean the kind of serious trouble there is going around these days."*

"I'll always wonder, though," Emily said, *"what they were doing that night the man fired his shotgun at them."*

"I never found out," I said, *"but they were a couple of scared kids all right."*

"And I'll never forget how eagerly they went to church the next morning," Emily said.

"What about tomorrow?" I asked. "Are they going to church tomorrow?"

"Of course they are. It's Easter—did you forget?"

"No, no," I said. "I just wondered if they were—you know, ready."

Emily looked at me and shook her head. "If attendance counts for anything, they're readier than you are."

⊰ XIV ⊱

*T*HE BOYS' MOTHER was still asleep when I woke up on Easter morning. So were the boys when I walked past their room on my way to the kitchen. The sunshine was streaming in the east windows, and I started humming as I lit the gas under the kettle. I would make coffee, I decided, and serve it in the bedroom. After that I would take on the formidable job of filling the boys with pancakes.

While I was waiting for the water to boil I began thinking about other Easters, and I remembered 1945, when I was overseas and the boys and their mother were at her parents' home in Vermont. That was the year Easter and April Fool's Day came on the same day, and though Chris got his head around the complication very quickly it took his four-year-old younger brother somewhat longer. They had been learning about Easter in their Sunday school, but when their grandfather started April Fool's Day routines at breakfast he confused Nick terribly.

As their mother wrote me, Nick got more and more worried as the jokes went on. He was still troubled when they arrived at church, and was deeply puzzled when he marched out with the Sunday school just before the sermon. But when his mother picked him up later at the parish house he was radiant. He had it all figured out.

"Mommy, do you know what?" he had said. "Well, there were these two women, see, and on Easter morning they went to the place where Jesus was buried and they wondered how they'd get that big rock rolled away from the door. Well, when they finally got there the rock was rolled away and Jesus was gone. Boy, Mommy, were those women fooled!"

I reminded his mother of the happening when I delivered the coffee, and we laughed about it all over again as we always do.

When the boys came to breakfast they were unusually bright and clean. They had on their Sunday suits and their white shirts. Their faces were scrubbed and their hair carefully combed in the intricate design that the current fashion demanded. Little dribbles of water and cream oil were visible on their foreheads. Chris had a small razor cut on his chin.

"What time do you have to be at church?" the boys' mother asked.

"He wants us half an hour early," Chris said. He explained that due to the enlarged choir there was some rehearsal necessary. "I'm going to be crucifer," he said.

"I'm going to be one of the altar boys," Nick said. "I

get to change the big prayer book from the Epistle side to the Gospel side."

"You're a good deal more interested in this church than in any one you ever went to before," I said. "How come?"

"Oh, I don't know," Chris said. "Father Blake makes us feel sort of as though he needed us."

"He says he doesn't know what he would do without us," Nick said.

"He does need you," the boys' mother said.

We left the house about nine. Chris drove carefully and not too fast. When we reached the church the boys went in through the choir-room door, and we parked under the elms along the street. We were gazing silently at the sunlit lawn and the ivy-covered redstone church when the boys' mother began laughing to herself.

"What?" I asked.

"Oh, I was thinking about when the boys were confirmed last year, and when we got home Nick said, 'Boy, I shouldn't have put all that lanolin cream oil on my hair. I bet the bishop's hands smelled like dead sheep.' "

"They certainly have had varied reactions to the religious experience," I said. "Remember what fun they had at Joey Levy's bar mitzvah?"

"They've had fun all right, but sometimes I wonder if we've been firm enough on matters like church and Sunday school."

"I think we have," I said. "Or maybe I should say, I think you have."

"That's the trouble," she said. "I'm always telling

them what they have to do, and you're always telling them to use their own judgment." She looked thoughtfully at me but then started laughing again.

"Now what?"

"I suddenly thought of the first Sunday school I didn't make them go back to because after they had been attending quite regularly for some time they came home and told me they didn't want to go back any more because they were tired of coloring Jesus."

"And don't forget the time they were practically kidnaped by a roving band of missionaries and taken to another Sunday school," I said. "What happened to that one?"

"That only lasted for a couple of Sundays," she said. "On the third Sunday somebody made a speech about how necessary it was to go into the highways and byways to seek out sinners for redemption. 'You must go gather in the sheaves,' he said, 'just the way we gathered in Chris and Nicky.'"

"You mean they didn't like being either sinners or sheaves?" I asked.

"Maybe," said their mother, "they didn't understand the figure of speech." She was quiet for a moment. "We've had a lot of Easters with the boys," she said. "I suppose we won't have many more."

I was watching the people entering the church. "We'd better go in," I said, "or we won't have this one. And I hope it's a good sermon."

On the way through the vestibule the boys' mother drew my attention to a sign tacked on the bulletin board. It was lettered by a shaky but obviously dedicated hand.

"Come to church regularly so that when you are *brought* in the Lord won't have to ask, 'Who is it?' "

We found seats and knelt for a minute. Lilies were banked around the cross on the altar, and their fragrance filled the church.

When the first chords of "Welcome, Happy Morning" sounded we stood up. The organ did not have a great voice, nor did any of the congregation, but the result was full and joyous.

Chris led the choir up the aisle. He was looking straight ahead as he passed us with his slow, measured step. Above the red cassock and the white surplice his face was serious and remote as it always is when he is concentrating. His hair was dry now and looked lighter. Nick walked with the altar boys in front of Father Blake, his face equally serious and intent, his eyes brown and level under his dark brows and hair.

Chris placed the cross at the end of the choir stalls and joined Nick at the altar. They knelt with the others for the opening prayer.

The Handel aria "Come Unto Him" was sung in a thin, sweet voice by a boy with the face of a young bulldog under his cropped bristly hair. When he was finished he sank into his seat with such a loud sigh of relief and pride that a silent laugh ran through the congregation.

After the solo Father Blake came down from the altar and stood facing us. "My sermon," he said, "is a line from a hymn we sing on Easter." Then he spoke his five-word sermon. " 'Every end is a beginning.' "

He stood quietly for a moment, turned back to the altar, and went on with the service.

As we watched the boys they looked so grown and re-moved that it was almost as if they were strangers, and when Chris led the choir down the aisle I felt that he and his brother not only were walking out of the church but might well be walking out of our lives.

I should have known better. As Chris passed us he winked. And as Nick went by he flashed us that quick, pleased grin that means he has just done something that he thinks is pretty good.

We paid our respects to Father Blake, complimented him on his service, and went to the car to wait for the boys.

"Were you thinking what I was thinking?" asked the boys' mother.

"Certainly," I said, "but I didn't weep about it."

"What was it that was bothering you, then?" she asked. "Hay fever?"

Chris and Nick came running across the lawn. They piled into the car, both talking at the same time.

"Is my brown button-down shirt clean?" Chris asked his mother, and, without waiting for an answer, turned to me. "Could I get an advance on my allowance? We want to go to the movies tonight."

At the same time Nick was saying, "Did you finish patching those old jeans of mine? Kenny and I are going camping, and do you know where my cooking kit is?"

"I'll have to be at my girl's house at eight," Chris said, "and you know my license doesn't let me drive after dark."

"Could I take the iron skillet with us?" Nick went on.

I looked at the boys' mother. "Cheer up," I said. "We're not through yet."

->>>->>>->>>-<<<-<<<-<<<

"Is that all?" Emily asked.

"Well," I said, "those are about all the parts that I can think of."

"It seems to me there are quite a lot of things you've left out, though," she said.

"Bound to be," I said. "Anything special?"

She looked away without answering. I saw that she did indeed have something particular in mind.

"What is it?" I asked.

"You didn't say anything at all about some of the bad times you and I have given each other."

"There weren't very many," I said, "and we kept them to ourselves at the time. Let's leave it that way."

Emily was silent. Then she said, "I guess you're right, but it doesn't make much of an ending."

"Sure it does," I said. "Remember the Easter sermon?"

"Of course I do," she said, "and I can see one kind of ending coming, but what is it the beginning of?"

"A hypotenuse," I said, "without a triangle."

"A what?" Emily asked. Then she smiled. "Oh, that. I don't think we have to worry about that."

Date Due

Ⓖ   PRINTED IN U. S. A.